For Betsy & Fred
With deep gratitude for everything

PROLOGUE

The scent of my blood was nauseating. Metallic, sweet and so strong. A blowfly moved across my cheek, but I felt nothing. It was soon joined by more. Above me, the crows and rooks shrieked in the tree tops.

I hover, I vibrate and I watch. I don't feel cold or hot or pain or any external feelings. But I am enveloped in sorrow. Clad in a coat of guilt, shod in regrets, alone in a great grey cloud of sadness. I remember, I love and I hate. No eyes, yet I watch. No ears, yet I hear. I hover and vibrate and watch and listen and remember and love and hate and sorrow.

I watched my murderer race away through the woods to where they had hidden their car. I followed in the wake of their wickedness as they dashed to my home.

The police and the press have come up with their versions of the Heronsford murders. But, if you tell the truth, you don't have to remember anything. I know the truth and need to tell it so I can forget.

My headlong race through the lanes to witness the harm that was to befall my family wasn't the beginning. The blood spilt in the woods, seen by the crows, wasn't the beginning either.

The beginning was a scene that resembled one of her

photographs. Beautiful but eerily still. She lay on her stomach, arms half extended. Long scarlet hair floating free, vivid against the turquoise blue beneath her. Small, pretty, tanned body enticing in a strappy pale top and dark blue shorts, shapely lower legs spread, one slightly bent. Dead.

1

---

22 JUNE

A wet spring had meant that weeds had kept returning to the border where the vigorous, peach-pink rambler spread itself up and across the south wall of her converted barn. The rose infused the air around it with an intense fruity scent.

Annie Berkeley was tackling the border now. The weeds were bigger and tougher to deal with than she usually allowed them to become, but the last couple of weeks had been so surprisingly hot that she had put off doing it. Her seventy-four-year-old back was aching and apart from that, she could have done with a cold flannel to run over her face and neck. Standing for a moment to relieve the pain, she thought of stopping on its account.

With only another couple of yards to go, she made the decision to continue. That she would be in more pain later, she balanced with the fact that at least the job would be done. She bent down to prise up a dock. A toad leapt over her hand and scuttled off. Annie flinched for a second only.

She stood up again, but the ache did not lessen. It was time, she decided, for a visit to Doctor Gordon.

She felt eyes on her, turned and saw her daughter waving at her from her office.

In the old stables that had been turned into offices, the tall skinny figure of Eliza Armstrong stood arms splayed, head bent over a large pine farmhouse table that was known as "the art table". Her almond-shaped green eyes scanned a batch of near identical photographic images scattered across its rectangular top.

There was something about her that might have reminded you of a gangly teenager. Her hips swayed slightly, the hem of her short green linen skirt swinging from side to side. If you had looked closely, you would have seen the iPod headphones under her generous head of wavy brown hair. You might also have picked up on her distraction and guessed that she would like to have avoided what she was doing.

Her task was to pick the best for the latest up-coming catalogue, and it was boring her. Her mind kept wandering towards what she would wear that evening. She wanted to look her best. He was going to be there. She thought about choosing the simple emerald green belted dress. It was a striking colour that she knew suited her. Then she considered the navy-blue blouse with tiny white stars paired with the white Bermuda shorts which did show off her long legs to advantage. Having plumped for the latter, when she came out of her reverie, a shot of guilt went through her for thinking such thoughts. She was married, for God's sake.

A thick clump of hair flopped forward over her long Modigliani face and she tossed her head back, straightening up as she did. In what had become an almost unconscious habit over time, she gathered and twisted her mane with one hand into a bunch at her nape. She crossed over to the desk where, with the other, she grabbed an elastic band from the misnamed desk tidy, expanded it with her fingers and slipped the clutch of hair through it. It was too hot for hair down.

Instead of returning to the table, she plopped her long body onto the expensive leather office swivel chair, bought when they had turned over their first fifty thousand pounds. With her feet, Eliza propelled herself and the chair across to the open window. She gazed across the wide stretch of the yard beyond where she saw the small purposeful figure of her mother, body bent and head bobbing as she weeded the flowerbed on the side of the barn, stopping occasionally to wipe the sweat from her forehead. She contemplated shouting to her to stop before she got sunstroke but thought better of it, especially since the usually sensible older woman was wearing a tatty old Panama that had belonged to Eliza's father.

A successful conversion twelve years before had turned the small barn into a two-bedroom modern house. It had once been a place where previous generations of her father's family of farmers had stashed hay and straw bales harvested from the pastures beyond. This had fed and bedded carriage horses, carthorses, hunters and children's ponies, once stabled where she was now sitting. That was when her parents had lived in Heronsford Manor Farm, the old brick and timber five-bedroom house. After her father had died, her mother had gifted the house to her only child, her husband Jay and their two children.

The sight of Jay walking towards the office diverted Eliza's attention. He was followed by the family's black Labrador. The man's head hung, his shoulders slumped, his gait was slow. He had become so different from the jaunty chap whose habitual, life-affirming stride was one of the many things she had found so touching about him. He was normally a positive-minded, go-ahead and forward-looking man, but the anxiety about the state of their business had affected him more deeply than Eliza would have believed possible. Even the clothes he was choosing to wear at the moment were the drabber, darker shirts and trousers, and dull grey T-shirts, when he had a raft of more interesting ones to choose from. Jay always had been a highly sensitive man who felt things deeply and took matters to heart, but lately, he had developed a preoccupied air that even the children had noticed.

Eleven years earlier, Jay had given up an extremely lucrative London job to spend more time at home with the family and to make a go of putting Eliza's name on the map as a ceramic designer. She had started as a hobby, making a pottery mug and a plate as a present for her mum. Everyone had liked them so much, they had encouraged her to make more and sell them locally. It had snowballed and soon she couldn't make enough. This had decided Jay to leave his job in the city and start Eliza Berkeley Designs with his own capital. They had worked extremely hard to get it off the ground. He had set up an earthenware pottery factory in Stoke-on Trent and invested heavily in promoting the brand. This had paid off well for the first few years, when people had flocked to buy Eliza's novel designs.

But in the last two to three years, the business had taken a major nosedive. This was not for lack of trying, because they had brought out new designs every year. It was more probably because the time for the middle classes to fill their kitchens with colourful, naïve images of farmyard animals, dogs and cats adorning chunky pottery mugs and plates, had had its day.

This year, Eliza had come up with some completely new ideas to try to boost the company's flagging sales. She and Jay had sat down to a brainstorming session to see what original and more current ideas they could come up with for the new catalogue. Eliza had hit on vegans and vegetarians as a growing trend among the chattering classes and her new collection was called "Fruit 'N' Veg".

At its zenith, the company turnover had been high. Most of this had been ploughed back into the business. But now those times were gone. The shops weren't stocking their goods anymore and now they were almost back to where they had started. Last year's turnover had been worryingly low. At the moment they were just surviving by selling old stock at much-reduced prices, but unless the new designs took off, the future looked grim. Eliza had come up with new ideas, different mug and teapot shapes, but for some reason they had not caught the imagination of the buyers who had usually stocked their products.

A free spirit at heart, Eliza would have been perfectly happy to muddle through in comparative poverty, or to have chucked it all in and done something else altogether, but her husband had so much to lose by letting the business go. If the new stock didn't sell, the writing would be on the wall and he would be forced to close down the factory. He dreaded the thought of having to put the potters, workers, managers and truck drivers out of work. What made it harder for him was that he had a love for the good things in life, cars, holidays, expensive wine, champagne, all the things that Eliza had never especially cared for, but that he hadn't had as a child and desperately wanted.

For the family's sake, Eliza had to try and keep cheerful about the situation. She was unsure whether they could rescue the business, but was determined not to let Jay or anyone know that she felt that way. At least, this is what she told herself, although there were times when she just wanted to run away from the business. And, it must be said, from Jay. But then surely everyone felt like that sometimes, and at the moment it was hardly surprising that she had the occasional fanciful thought.

Eliza took a last glance back at her mum slowly straightening up, a trug full of weeds in one hand, the other rubbing an evidently hurting back. She sighed in the knowledge that lately the old girl did seem to be slowing up and developing aches and pains.

But Eliza had an unusual mix between a practical approach to life coupled with an imaginative, idealistic nature. She told herself to remember that age happens and that since the once so energetically formidable woman was now seventy-four years old, such things were to be expected.

At that moment, as though aware of her daughter's gaze, her mother looked up and waved at Eliza. It was too far to shout. She mimicked drinking from a cup, pointed to her house and held up four fingers to suggest four o'clock. Eliza gestured back with thumbs up.

She had hardly seen or talked to her in the last few days and was happy to accept the offer.

As Jay stepped through the door, Eliza arranged her face in its latest go-to expression of what she hoped was a broad, encouraging smile. At least it was Friday. Perhaps meeting up later with their mates would cheer him up. As they often did on Friday evenings, they were convening in the Old Cock at seven o'clock. Knocking back a few and unwinding before the weekend invariably turned into a boozy time since none of them were known for holding back. Eliza held an affection for all of them, although Louise Ryan could be tricky and irritatingly flirtatious with the men – which included Jay, who seemed to relish it. That morning she had made a huge Bolognese that would be a filler over the weekend for hungry souls coming and going, so if they decided to eat at the pub that evening, there would be food for Juliet, their seventeen-year-old, who was quite capable of feeding herself. Their eleven-year-old daughter Holly was staying the night with a school friend, so the parents could leave Juliet to her own devices.

At around four o'clock, Eliza left the office and her distracted husband to cross the fifty-odd metres to Manor Farm Barn. She rapped on the door and entered at the same time.

Her mother's elderly fawn pug Mildred danced over to greet Eliza, her front legs high-stepping, her bottom wiggling its corkscrew tail in delight. Eliza bent down and made a fuss of her. Annie's sparky blue eyes vanished into crinkly slits across her face and a broad smile spread across it as she got up from her ancient yellow armchair. The stiffness evident in her movement, she gave her daughter a bear hug before going into her kitchen to switch on the kettle. A feeling of release went through Eliza's body and she felt her shoulders drop. It felt good to bask in the absolute love of her mother's warmth, and her exasperation with the situation she and Jay were going through temporarily melted away.

She watched her mother's painful progress and reflected that lately she seemed to have aged. It wasn't the short white hair that gave this impression – she'd had that for the last ten years – it was more about the way she looked and moved. "Your back's pretty bad, isn't it?"

"No, no, not that bad, just a bit stiff when I garden, that's all."

Typical of her mother, who deliberately avoided the reality of ageing. Eliza may have understood why once so remarkable a force would find it hard to come to terms with the fact, but it was still irritating. Besides, it was more than likely to be arthritis that could be treated.

In a firm tone she said, "Mum, go and see Edward. He'll give you something for it." Edward Gordon, the village doctor had been at Heronsford surgery for as long as Eliza could remember. He was a family friend and when his wife had died of a brain tumour, Annie had been one of the kinder and more reliable people to have helped get him through a dreadful time.

"You're quite right. I've been meaning to, it's just a matter of getting around to it."

"I'm ringing him on Monday morning and taking you to see him next week. It's so silly to suffer unnecessarily. I'll bring some ibuprofen over, it should help ease the ache."

"You know I'm not keen on pills, darling–"

Her daughter interrupted her, "That's plain silly, Mum. You're in pain and that's what they are for."

"All right, well maybe I'll try one. I promise I'll call Edward myself and see him next week."

"Take two..." said Eliza, "...and good."

Relaxing on the scruffy old blue floral sofa that had once been in the farm sitting room and part of her life since she could remember, Eliza scanned the old pale grey and light-brown oak rafters that curved up to meet in the middle of the barn ceiling. The strains of Yo-yo Ma playing Bach filled the high space with a mournful glory. An ancient cello propped against a corner wall advertised the fact that her mother, something of a hobby cellist herself, was a devotee of the instrument. She still played sometimes. It was silently acknowledged among others that she was no virtuoso. In fact, hearing her play could make for difficult listening to both trained and untrained ears. Once heard, it was unusual for repeat requests. But the old girl did so love it, which was after all the point.

Her mother often got on her nerves. Eliza convinced herself it was largely because they now lived so close and saw so much of one another. The reality was that throughout her life as an adult, refusing to see it, Eliza had actually felt split between a deep love for and a sense of distance from and difference to the only parent she'd had since her father had died when she was fifteen. It had never been easy having a mother praised by all, who was both more academic and more useful to others than her daughter believed she could ever have hoped to be.

Her occasional irritation had grown worse these days. Seeing her mother slowly declining before her eyes uncovered a fear within her she had no desire to acknowledge. Perhaps it was her mother's innate strength that she was scared of losing. This had, after all, pulled her through the grief of losing her father.

Annie handed her a plate of Rich Tea biscuits. They were the only ones she ever bought. She considered the rest an extravagance. Although she really didn't like them, Eliza took one to gratify. She noticed that, unusually, her mum didn't.

Like a magnet, Mildred was at her feet, snorting and snuffling, expectant eyes popping, toad-like mouth grinning in the dark wrinkles of the short-muzzled face. Mildred was much spoiled and it was understood she was allowed a biscuit if she stayed on the floor. When younger, the children, who loved their grand-mother, used as they were to the luxury of biscuits with chocolate coatings and cream middles, had also taken the occasional Rich Tea to please. While Annie wasn't looking, most of them were hastily dispatched into the ever-obliging chops of Mildred. These days, they'd had enough of endurance and when offered, they simply said no, though always politely. Eliza slipped most of the biscuit to Mildred, whose eating habits did not make enjoyable viewing.

"Like the kurta, Mum. Good colour." Her mother was wearing a coral-pink top.

"Thank you. Yes, rather cheerful, isn't it? I got it in a sale last July and it's proving very useful in this hot weather."

Annie was extremely fond of colour. Short of stature and well-covered, she tended to wear bright loose tunics, kaftans, kurtas or tops along with scarves of many varieties and long skirts or smart trousers. Her shoes were usually cheerful shades or, if duller, adorned with buttons, bows or buckles. She generally favoured medium heels to give her a bit of extra height. Today, her shoes were unusual flat slip-ons with thin, multi-coloured stripes.

Her garden had a similar theme and was something of a clutter of colour. She mixed old-fashioned roses with flowering shrubs and herbaceous plants of every kind, accounting for all the seasons from yellow winter jasmine to autumn bulbs from bright pink nerines to red autumn dahlias. There was always something in bloom.

Annie noticed how tired her daughter looked, but decided that to mention it would not be helpful. She settled back into her armchair and carefully avoided talking about the state of the company, instead directing the conversation to Juliet's A-level exams and her choices of potential universities. Juliet was hoping to get into Bristol. She would finish her A-levels by mid-June.

Having asked how Eliza was enjoying her sculpting course, Annie, unable to resist, let drop how strained Jay seemed. She knew a lot about the man's history. His childhood had been difficult and had resulted in a reticence he had tried his hardest to contest as an adult. In this, he mostly succeeded, but his exterior generally hid an uneasiness that, despite his best efforts, would appear from time to time.

It suddenly occurred to Annie that there was something helpful she could do. "Would it help if I slept at the farm to look after Juliet and Holly so you two can take a much-needed holiday?"

"Thanks," said Eliza. "Not at the moment. I wish he'd go off on his own for a while."

Annie wasn't surprised by this response. The tension was showing in both their faces. The marriage had been a success until the recent debacle with the company had put excessive demands on it. Jay was proving to lack the emotional strength to deal with it.

Annie prayed they would find a way through the current mess since both their lives were so tied up with the business. It was also much in her interest that they should. She wanted things to stay as they were. For if Jay and Eliza split up, what would become of Manor Farm? Planning rules meant that the house and the barn would have to be sold as a single property, so she would have to move if they did. After all, she had given them the property on the understanding that she would remain there until her death.

Mother and daughter chatted for a while until Eliza stood up and said, "Juliet will be home, better go. Sunday lunch as usual?"

She kissed her mother, adding, "Up to anything scandalous I should know about, Mother?"

"If you call having Pam Sowerby for a drink at 6.30 scandalous, then scandalous I intend to be, which may include slugging down a bit of the hard stuff while playing chess." Annie would go a long way for a game of chess.

"Good on you, Mum. Give her my love." Eliza blew her another kiss and left the barn with no idea that Sunday lunch would be very far from usual.

2

22 JUNE

If you had been waiting on the Liverpool Street station platform for the 11.44am train that day, you would definitely have noticed the black-haired forty-something woman in the tight-fitting blue dress, the floppy red straw hat and the highest pair of red heels. You might even have recognised Francesca Bianchi from her many appearances in TV dramas.

Although a pretty woman, Francesca turned heads more for her fame, her flamboyance and her curvaceous figure as she tottered along pulling a suitcase on wheels beside her. During the first decade of the twenty-first century, she had done a long stint on the soap opera, *Castleton*, in which she had played the much loved bar lady of the local pub. In a sense, she had been playing herself, although the part had not started out that way. As the scriptwriters had grown to know and love the actress, they had written the part to suit her natural outgoing, sexy, dramatic character.

Francesca had spent the past three nights with her parents in London and was glad to be going home to Heronsford, to Smith's Cottage and to Thai, her beloved Siamese cat. She was anticipating "tying a few on" in the pub that evening with some of her local pals.

Well-loved in the village, her celebrity status made her the local star, a thing she much enjoyed.

An Italian by birth, Francesca's restaurateur parents had moved to the UK when she was a two-year-old in 1980. The following year they had opened Fredo's in London's South Kensington. The restaurant's fame had grown until the place had been booked solid daily. The energetic little character of the pretty, funny, dark-haired child with almost black eyes had relished the attention of diners at the restaurant. To the amusement of Londoners unused to seeing young children in restaurants, she had been allowed the run of the place. Growing up an only child in such circumstances had led her first to enjoy, then to seek the limelight in her career. Fortunately, this quest had been coupled with a generous talent for acting at school. Having been taken under the wing of an eager drama teacher who had encouraged her in this direction, she had won a place at the Royal Central School of Speech and Drama. She had done well there and had picked up a few West End roles including two that had been starring, one receiving an *Evening Standard* award for best actress in a Shakespeare play.

Francesca loved acting but aside from that, adult life had not been quite the sparkling event she had hoped for. A marriage at the age of twenty-three and a bad choice of husband had given her a discrete but powerful insecurity that life had hitherto spared her. A good-looking, wild young actor had turned out to be about as self-centred as a person can be. Constantly cheating on her with other women, Tom had finally ditched her for a richer one after only six years. He had left her with a deep resentment and a newly discovered jealous side.

Blessed with a resourceful nature, Francesca had soon got back on her feet, but boyfriends had come and gone, partly as she never found a man she had loved enough, but partly as a result of her newly formed trust issues. In due course, she had resorted to help from the bottle and in spending more time at Smith's Cottage, her little thatched number at the west end of Heronsford.

The two-bedroomed cottage had a pretty garden and was in a one-way lane overlooking open fields to the back. When Tom had a role at the Cambridge Arts Theatre, Francesca had stayed with him in lodgings for the play's pre-London run of two weeks. The couple had liked Cambridge and, in spite of, or because of its flatness, the area around it. In an impetuous moment when driving through a sprawling village about eight miles south of Cambridge, they had been entranced by Heronsford's winding lanes and mix of houses from Tudor to Victorian, from ancient thatched cottages to modern estates. When they had seen tiny Smith's Cottage for sale, explored some more to find a village shop, two pubs and a railway station, it was a done deal. They had bought the delightful cottage as a weekend getaway. Although it had been inexpensive, it had polished off any spare funds they had shared. For a while this had not mattered but when Tom had left, they had divided what was left. Tom had taken the small London flat and she, the cottage. There was always room at her parents' for when she was in London.

Although she protested to the contrary, Francesca had a deep inner sadness that since then she had found no-one with whom to have children. When girlfriends suggested she became a single mother, she airily laughed it off saying that the time for such things had passed and that anyway, she was not prepared to give up her career to have a child. And this was true. She had now got so used to her independence that she had put the idea out of her mind.

The yellow number this evening, she thought. Strongly tanned, she knew she looked especially desirable in that dress. Good-looking Patrick Ryan was going to be there and the two of them enjoyed a secret flirtation that might have led to an affair, had Francesca not been a good friend of his wife Louise. Still, that didn't stop her adding an extra wiggle to her walk when Patrick was around and as a result of the secret Louise had recently let her in on, she was beginning to think that what had seemed unfeasible might now become a real possibility. And this excited her.

3

22 JUNE

"I'm meeting the usual suspects in the Old Cock this evening." Bob McKenzie looked directly into his wife's eyes. "Don't suppose you want to come, do you, Stella?"

This was his method of putting words in her mouth, so she had no need to say much except that she'd rather not go. She would just have to sit there as usual while Bob flirted with other women. For Bob, it didn't matter much since he would do his own thing whether Stella was with him or not. But he would prefer not to have her with him.

A solid, chunky man who stood around five foot seven with grey eyes and thick mousey-blond hair that curled over his collars and was balding in the middle, Bob had a broad fleshy face, a firm square jaw and above it a wide, thick-lipped, almost effeminate mouth. "Bonker Bob", as he had been dubbed by amused friends who had watched him seduce woman after woman, had been a mover and shaker on the Cambridge social scene and to a lesser degree in London until he had hit forty years old.

Then he had bought Heronsford Manor, a beautiful eight-bedroom red brick house built in early Georgian times. When the house had been given to McKenzie's to market, Bob had immediately snapped it up at a deliberately undervalued price.

He had put in an indoor heated swimming pool in what was once the conservatory while the room next door had a movie screen on the wall with twenty cinema seats installed. The billiards room still housed a full-size table. There was even a gym installed in one of the old outbuildings. The estate retained two crop-growing fields and a large amount of woodland that encircled the house. Bob loved shooting and was even a fair shot. He had his own winter shoot in the estate-owned Newman's Wood where the gamekeeper raised pheasants.

Having bought the manor, Bob had needed a woman to both run the house and to adorn it. Not being one for halves, he had got himself two. A highly efficient live-in housekeeper-cook was soon followed by the ravishing Stella who he moved in to share his "life of a gentleman". He had met her one evening in a famous London West End nightclub. She was the girl so many men wanted. Using the charm and flashing the money that many females found irresistible, he had wooed and beguiled the inexperienced twenty-one-year-old into falling for him.

Tall, blonde and a beautiful young Swedish model, Stella had a body that left most men dumbstruck. A stereotype maybe, but a dream one as far as men were concerned.

Although Stella played the role of adoring, dutiful wife, she had been brought up in a large noisy family and she missed them. But she hadn't so much fallen as tripped headlong for Bob, and if you fell for him, it was clear you had to accept all that came with him. He was charismatic, charming, cool under pressure, focused, energetic, impulsive and had a hard-nosed toughness along with a natural gift for leadership.

Stella understood all this as well as being very aware of his possessive, adoring, controlling nature when it came to her. She knew that her husband's voracious appetite for sex and his love of women might encompass others beside herself, but it was a subject she avoided talking to Bob about. And as for the other women in the village, well, they seemed to have closed ranks against her.

4

22 JUNE

Katie Nicholson stepped into the shower. She turned the taps until the water spouted lukewarm. *Why, oh blooming why,* she asked herself as it splashed over her dark blonde bob and down her back, *does this keep happening?* She had been so careful all week to have no more than a glass of red with her evening meal and hadn't broken her promise to herself except once. But here she was, yet again letting herself down.

If you had met her you would have understood that for Katie to attempt to keep up with her husband Hamish's bon vivant enjoyment of food and drink, was daft. His large six foot three inch frame was considerably better able to hold its alcohol than Katie's five foot three inches. But then, Katie wasn't the world's brightest. She made up for this in many respects by finding most things funny, by being an accommodating, loving wife, a good cook and fun to be with. You would call her an outgoing personality and to back this up, she was a great thrower of parties. But deep inside herself, she knew perfectly well why sometimes she drank to excess. She knew too that others thought her a bit thick. She did in fact have a much higher intelligence than she was given credit for, but for her own reasons, found it easier if people didn't notice. It did, after all, encourage a lack of expectation from others and this helped smooth her path through life.

When she was six, while she had been sitting in the back of the car, her mother and father had both died in a hideous accident in a motorway pile-up.

Only mildly injured but in deep shock, Katie had been rescued from the car and taken to hospital to recover. Her grandparents had come to her side and she had ended up living with them for the rest of her unusual childhood. While she had felt loved, she had also felt she had been cheated and had missed out. When her grandfather had died too, she had been certain that death was out to haunt her for the rest of her life, and no amount of counselling once she was older had helped dispel her feeling of doom.

Her rich grandmother had done everything she could for her, and Katie had never wanted for any material thing. She had been sent to boarding school because her grandmother had the sense to understand that, much as Katie needed her, she also needed to get away from her and learn independence.

When Katie left school, she had done a cookery course at an expensive cookery school in London while she had shared a flat with some other friends from school.

There she had met and fallen in love with Hamish. They had fallen into an on and off relationship. The off times had been when Hamish had felt mildly panicked about committing himself to remain faithful to one girl for evermore. He was, after all, a man who loved the girls, and at those times there had seemed just too many lovely ones to have to choose one alone.

Their fate had been settled when Katie had become pregnant. Whether or not by mistake, no-one was sure. But that she adored Hamish was not in doubt. That he had loved her was not either.

Anyway, for a good egg like Hamish who could always be relied on and who loved children, it had been a no brainer. They had decided to bring up their child (and hopefully future children) in as rural an environment as they could find. Coming across Wood Farm for sale with McKenzie's, they had fallen in love with it straightaway. Originally, the smallholding had been part of the Heronsford Manor Estate where Eliza's ancestor Berkeleys had lived. In Victorian times, her great-great grandfather who had been brought up to expect to take over running the estate, had decided he much preferred landscape painting and collecting butterflies. His failure to keep an eye on the management of the large amount of land had meant that, before long, the family had fallen on what they would have called "hard times". This had forced the Berkeleys to sell off most of the thousand acres of land and the big house, retaining Manor Farm for the family to live in, along with about sixty acres. The Manor had changed hands a few times since then and when Bob McKenzie had bought it, he in turn had sold off the Gate Lodge, Wood Farm and most of the remaining acreage at a good profit.

A narrow dead-end lane, Wood Lane led to the old rear lodge house and beyond it to Wood Farm. This was all the better as far as Hamish and Katie Nicholson were concerned, since they loved being away from people and close to nature. Hamish was a Scotsman who had been brought up in the highlands, so a love of the countryside ran deep through his veins. As its name suggested, the house was surrounded by woodland on three sides. This had been neglected for years and gradually encroached on what had once been the farmyard of the smallholding. When the Nicholsons bought it, they cleared enough of it to make a large garden, a small paddock, and for the sun to reach the house.

The woods behind them ended at a narrow crop field. On the opposite edge of which was the back of Rooks Wood that was part of Manor Farm. The Nicholsons kept chickens and Hamish had dug a pond on which wild ducks and moorhens had taken up residence. Their ever-growing vegetable garden with two greenhouses was his pride. The couple both loved cooking and experimented with home-made sauces, jams, chutneys and Katie became brilliant at home-made ice creams. Hamish produced delicious fruited gins and vodkas, always popular with their pals. They had even experimented with old-fashioned home-made wines such as parsnip and elderflower, Hamish's most recent being beetroot. Contrary to what you might assume from where they had chosen to live, they were social beings and often invited friends to stay for weekends as well as befriending others from the neighbourhood.

Hamish had played rugby for his school and then been to Lough-borough University. On the rugby pitch he had been renowned for his courage – thought by some to err on the edge of foolishness – and but for a shoulder injury, he had been tipped to go on to play for Saracens or one of the other big clubs in the rugby premiership league.

In much the same way that he had been the first to tackle in a game of rugby, Hamish was the type to throw himself heartily into a job. Brook's, the East Anglian real ale brewery where he worked, was based in Bury St Edmunds. Like Jay and Eliza's business, it was suffering. This may partly have been to do with the poor state of the national economy that was affecting businesses across the land. While the country was not in recession, newspapers and other media were painting a picture that it was teetering on the brink. Local ales might sell well when the nation is prospering but once a fad died down, the smaller brewers seldom made much profit. These beers were more expensive than the big nationals, who either bought the brewers out or they went out of business.

Hamish had begged the board to modernise its ancient brewing equipment and introduce new products but the chairman and managing director, both beyond retirement age, had stood firmly against change.

Hamish was quietly looking for a new job. But he was not finding it easy, so for the meanwhile had to remain with Brook's.

Driving home that evening, Hamish felt the longed-for 'Friday relief' that the weekend lay ahead. He and Katie were meeting some friends at the village pub. Looking forward to letting his hair down, he was particularly glad that Jay and Eliza Armstrong were going, particularly Eliza, who was a special woman and one who always cheered him up. He was fond of Jay too, but the man had been such a grumpy chap lately, and didn't seem to realise how lucky he was to have such a lovely wife, nor to appreciate her as he should.

5

22 JUNE

Eliza heard the crunch of Juliet's bike wheels on the gravel and knew it was time to stop work. Her daughter would be hot and tired after the train journey from Cambridge and the ride back from Heronsford station, so she gave her a few minutes to get a drink of water and take a breath before joining her in the sitting room.

Juliet was immersed in her laptop on the sofa. Eliza sat down next to her and draped an arm around her shoulders. "Holly is away on a sleepover and we're joining some mates at the pub this evening. You are very welcome to join us, but since I am sure it will be the last thing you would want to do, there's a large bowl of Bolognese in the fridge and you know where the spaghetti is."

"Can I have him over?"

She was seventeen. Eliza accepted that she and her boyfriend were likely to be having sex. She and Jay did not yet allow them to share a bedroom or spend nights together. He was, after all, only seventeen himself and they were both still at school. Juliet was on the pill so there should be no worries there, but her parents didn't want to make it too easy or cosy – where was the fun in that? Besides, this September Juliet would be off to university and they didn't want her having to deal with a broken heart before she went. There would likely be enough of that sort of thing once she got there.

Eliza stroked her child's glossy brown hair.

"Of course. But you know the rules."

"Great. His mum will bring him over, at least she usually does." She was already texting with dexterous speed.

"Okay for him to stay until eleven thirty?"

"Fine. Give him some spag bol too. See you later. Have fun and don't do anything I wouldn't do..." She gave her daughter an arch wink that Juliet didn't notice, her head buried in messages winging to and fro.

The hot air was thick with the scent of elderflowers that had won the battle for hedgerow space with a few overshadowed pink and white dog roses. Without speaking, Eliza and Jay strolled along the riverside of the rutted, pot-holed dead-end lane from their house to the village.

Not afraid of silence, they were both relieved to get away from the office. On the other side of the lane, speckled with ox-eye daisies, buttercups, purple knapweed and loosestrife, the verge tumbled down to the river, shallow from the dry, hot weather. Once the rains returned, it would fill up again to get up a proper flow. It was on its way to join the Cam and divided the lane from a broad view of the surrounding countryside stretching into a distance virtually un-punctured by hills. This was the world that Eliza knew gave her safety and contentment.

She crossed over to walk along the river's edge. Ever since a small girl, she had been interested in wild flowers and learning their names. Their various colours and shapes fascinated her and sometimes she wished she had studied to become a gardener or botanist. She was never happier than when studying the form of a flower head or its manner of spreading its genes. She may have picked this up from her mother or it was simply part of her nature. Being an only child, flowers had been her friends, as had the trees that grew around the farm.

A wonderful old pink chestnut tree on the left of the house spread thick comforting branches low, one that held an ancient swing and a thick rope with a knot in the bottom. Her father had played on it as a child, followed by his daughter Eliza and then, with a replacement swing put up by Jay, Juliet and Holly in their turn. For purely sentimental reasons, the two mothers appreciated this continuity of time.

A long snake uncoiled in front of Eliza's foot and she shrieked as it slithered its way through the undergrowth to hurtle down into the river and swim a rapid, undulating path through the water. Shuddering with dislike for the creature, she stopped for a moment to regain her composure. As so often these days, Jay, wandering along the middle of the lane, was in some reverie of his own and failed to notice.

In a few minutes, Jay and Eliza reached Mill Road where the main village started and they walked along the long curve that went left again, passing some fine Georgian, Victorian and plaster-painted Tudor houses in the traditional East Anglian hues of warm creams, soft pale pinks, peach and bull's blood. Further along they turned once more, right down Church Lane where thatched cottages were interspersed with twentieth century private and pre- and post-war brick council houses. They passed the generous village green that included a cricket pitch beyond which sat a small stone church with a solid comforting Norman tower entirely spoiled by the later addition of an out-of-place, too-narrow lead spire, like an upturned ice cream cone had dropped onto it from the sky.

Frowning, Jay suddenly spoke. "Hope Bob doesn't mention Scotland this evening. It's usually around this time he puts out the invite."

"Why don't you go, Jay? You love it and it's not much to pay for such a good time."

"We're simply not in the position to take holidays at the moment." He pulled crossly at the collar of his T-shirt. "We've had plenty in the past and it really won't hurt us."

She noticed his clenched hands.

"Besides, what about you? You need a break too, Eliza."

Such a change had come over the man once so free with spending his money. It was so sad. Eliza glanced sideways at him. She nudged him.

"The whole situation doesn't worry me as much as it worries you and, as you also know, I am always happy as Larry simply to be at home. The point is that you, my darling, are in dire need of a break. You've been working so hard and I wonder if you realise how tense you are? A week away from all the worry could be the recharge you need. Besides, of course we can afford it."

The truth is, they both needed a break from work and one another. Jay's face flushed.

"That's not the point. I cannot just walk away for a week at the moment. The catalogue is ready for release and I need to oversee it. I cannot take time off until I have done everything to get some sales. I refuse to spend money on my pleasure when I have to think about school fees and university costs for Juliet. I'm not sure you fully realise the trouble we are in, Eliza. We have virtually no capital left and almost nothing coming in." His voice rose. "We have to start understanding that we can't go on the way we always have. If things don't pick up very soon, we may have to consider selling up."

"Selling up? Never! I won't... we can't sell up. What about Mum? She gave us the house, remember? The children can go into state school." Not so calm now, Eliza added, "In fact, it would be good for them. Give them a dose of reality. I was never in favour of sending them to these expensive schools. And now it has caught up with us. Just because you went to private sch–" she stopped herself.

Unlike most of her local peers, the children of the well-off middle classes who were family friends, at her mother's insistence, Eliza had been state-educated at an excellent school in a nearby town. This she had never regretted and was proud of.

"At this stage? You can't be serious?" He looked aghast.

Her tone was shrill. "Why the fuck not? I was at one, let me remind you!" They were nearing the pub. She stopped walking and calmed herself. "Look, Jay, now is really not the time, is it? For this evening shall we try to forget about it and do our best to enjoy ourselves? We can talk about it tomorrow."

He shrugged and they retreated back into silence. How could she be so immune to what was happening to them? Didn't she realise that they had invoices to pay, workers to take care of, tax bills to settle? The council tax, the school fees, the problems owning sixty acres brought with it. The worst of it was that having been gifted the farm, they couldn't really sell it – especially while Annie B. was still alive.

A thick roof of thatch, low ceilings and walls yellowed with the stain of years of nicotine, dark stone floors that had resisted change through the years, its atmosphere and the landlord, were the reasons people drank in the Old Cock. The subject of many ribald jokes, this was an ancient coaching inn. To make any pub pay its way, it had to concede to modern times by producing a small half-hearted menu from which you could choose a ploughman's, a tuna and mayo or a ham and tomato baguette, a hamburger and chips or a sandwich.

Jay needed to duck as they went through the low front door and up to the bar. Hung along the top with ancient pewter tankards, old oak beams covered the low ceiling in front of a wide inglenook fireplace. Above this, another long, gnarled and darkened beam supported mellow terracotta handmade bricks either side. Old pewter plates and toby mugs were displayed along its top. The landlord looked up from scribbling an order in front of a waiting group of customers. He raised a hand, blew a kiss and mouthed hello.

An old man was perched on a stool beside the bar and a pair of unavoidable watery blue eyes in sagging sacks of old flesh fastened on Jay and Eliza. They belonged to an ex-army widower, the pub's main fixture and storyteller. Fortunately for other pub-goers, he was long past expecting responses from people. Without the need to listen, the occasional nod from those too stunned to attempt a gap in his cheerful waffle would suffice to keep him happy as he blathered on. When he got on to Aden, it generally proved too much to bear so there was always a horseshoe of space around him. The landlord and other bar staff, apart from fetching him his usual pints, didn't acknowledge him at all. It may sound cruel, but it wasn't. It was self-defence on the part of people who otherwise might have lost the will to survive. The old boy simply didn't notice.

He swivelled his body towards Jay and Eliza and started off on what would be a never-ending tale of his childhood in the Raj. They were only saved by the arrival of Katie and Hamish Nicholson. Homer, their ill-trained manic cocker spaniel was on a lead but tripping everyone up and misbehaving as usual. Bob McKenzie followed a few minutes later and last, as always, but glamorous as ever, Francesca Bianchi.

Hugs and handshakes done between the friends, removing her sunglasses with exaggerated emphasis and planting a huge kiss on the main fixture's hard, red-veined cheek, Francesca said, "Lovely to see you, darling."

The monologue ceased for a moment and before the old boy could take up his story again, the friends grabbed the chance and disappeared as fast as possible. They had gone into the unprepossessing triangular garden where, against an old brick wall on one side, a few sad flowers hung their heads between bedraggled weeds that bordered the edge of a patchy lawn so parched it had turned biscuit colour. A low, shabby picket fence bordered the roadside. But it was not for beauty or serenity that people came to this pub. It was for its fine cask ales, its friendly landlord, its atmosphere of age and lack of pretension. The women found a large picnic table with benches attached at its sides and an open parasol slotted through a hole in its middle.

Bob, Jay and Hamish made their orders as fast as they could and Bob carried a tray of bottles of wine and beer to the table, followed by Hamish and Jay carrying the glasses. Realising they weren't at the bar any more, the main fixture lifted his beer mug in a toast that they neither saw nor heard.

In keeping with his flamboyant personality, Bob was wearing a white baseball cap and a bright Hawaiian short-sleeved-shirt of orange and turquoise that did him absolutely no favours.

But at least, thought Eliza, *he has chosen beige shorts. And he's not wearing socks with sandals.* Why, she wondered, did Stella, who had such good taste in clothes, have such a lack of influence over what Bob wore? Didn't she have any control over him at all?

When he chose to, Bob could be very smartly dressed since he went to Saville Row in London's West End to have suits, tweed jackets and twill trousers made. But unlike the genuine old suited and booted characters that had always frequented his long-established tailor, Bob chose the most striking fabrics they stocked. His jackets and coats invariably lined in bright coloured silks or satins. And if he wore a striped suit, it would be a chalk stripe as noticeable as he could find with perhaps a yellow or bright purple lining.

In truth, Eliza decided, what let down Bob's attempts to seem like an upper class gentleman was his lack of subtlety. *None of it matters,* she thought. *That's what is so silly, as no-one except Bob cared about what impression he gave.*

"Stella's got a cold, so she's gone to bed," he said by way of apology for her absence.

"Oh, what bad luck to get a cold in June. That's really unusual," said Katie. And everyone murmured appropriate things. Although, in truth, nobody would feel her absence much. Stella often avoided coming to the pub and when she did, she rarely contributed to the conversation or to the group's fun. Bob was the extrovert and leader of that partnership. He was hugely entertaining and fun to be with while

Stella sat around looking beautiful, elegant, soigné and somehow disconnected from them all.

You only had to look at her to guess she might have been a model. She seemed like a fish out of water and it was agreed among these country people, with their gardens that mattered so much to them and their dogs and their love of all things rural, that the poor girl who was not even in her own country, was clearly a city girl at heart, not a bit suited to country life.

Francesca, Eliza and Katie had made continuous efforts to be friendly. But younger than them by a decade, Stella had barely responded to their kind-hearted overtures and so they had more or less given up making them. It wasn't that they disliked her – there was really nothing about her to dislike. They just didn't warm to her much as she gave them so little to work with.

It was only Francesca, who chatted to her about London and fashion and shops and restaurants, with whom she had some rapport.

Katie tugged and pushed at Homer's backside to get him to lie still under the table. The cocker had other things in mind, especially a collie that was lying quietly by its owner's side while he drank his beer at another table. The dog only ever did as it was told for a maximum of two minutes. The other women wished Katie had left the little blighter at home.

Bob set down the tray on the table. "Here you go, ladies."

Bob's slightly obvious attempts to seem middle or even upper class were happily forgiven, as was the fact that he loved to show off his racy cars and extravagantly furnished house. He threw wonderful dinner parties that always ended up in his swimming pool. Then there was tennis in the summer on the immaculately kept grass court. Bob was generous with his money in an ostentatious way.

"Bob insisted on buying us bottles instead of glasses of wine," said Jay, and Eliza could tell he was put out. He had always hated being upstaged by other men, calling it bad mannered, although the fact that he minded so deeply said more about his egotism than his comprehension of etiquette. Jay sat down opposite Katie with Hamish between him and Eliza.

There was a chorus of thank yous at which Bob waved an airy hand, "*No es nada.*"

Eliza and Hamish swapped amused glances. Certainly they were hypocrites since they secretly spoke of their disapproval for Bob's showy lifestyle but were quick to attend his parties and receive his generosity and hospitality. But for all this insincerity, they never let Bob get an inkling and they did in fact both like and admire the man whose charm could mesmerise and whose wit was quick.

He squashed himself between Francesca and Katie. "Budge up, you beautiful creatures. Make room for your favourite man."

Francesca, darkly tanned in a low-cut sleeveless yellow dress and highly unsuitable blue stilettos, swished along the bench until she was comfortable. Taking off her large pair of sunglasses again, she puckered her carefully pencilled eyebrows, rolled her heavily kohled dark brown eyes heavenwards and, leaning slightly forwards, addressed the audience. "Ask me who has had," she deployed a dramatic pause, "the worst fucking week ever?"

They all kept straight faces. Nobody was willing to feed her the line until Hamish took pity. "Okay then, sweetie, who?"

"Me, darling, fucking me. That is who."

"Fucking you?" said Bob. "I can oblige there, no trouble, sweetie. But when, my little Itie, when? This evening?"

"Oh, Bob, if only it weren't for Stella, you know I would simply love to, darling."

The worst week ever turned out to be that Francesca had been distraught because Thai the cat had gone missing for twenty-four hours but returned the next day.

The other contributing factors to her terrible week were a broken high heel in Charing Cross (it was not explained what she was doing there) and turning up for what had transpired was the wrong day for an audition.

This, the others suspected to be the result of self-induced memory loss due to too much alcohol. But the reality was that, in spite of her predilection for a drink or fourteen, when it came to her career, Francesca was able to put drink aside and function surprisingly well.

Francesca's theatrical exaggerations were something the group of friends actually delighted in as, fully aware of herself, Francesca was thoroughly good at deliberate self-parody. She was so warm, outgoing, sweet-hearted and amusing that most people loved her, though some found her too much. And she was, after all, an actress, albeit not quite landing the roles she once had. The friends suspected this was down to her drinking habits. But they had all seen her in a London play some years before, for which she had received good reviews. And they watched avidly when she had various parts on television, series and plays.

Francesca enjoyed and made much of the fact of her profession for these non-theatre friends. There was always her latest theatre story that frequently made everyone howl with laughter, along with the fact that the drunker she became, the funnier it made her. A keen cook whose weight and curves did not worry her, like she crammed herself into tight clothes, she also loved to cram friends into Smith's Cottage to eat delicious Italian food learnt from her childhood in Fredo's.

Lately, she seemed to be at the cottage more. Her friends worried that the parts were starting to dry up.

In response to Francesca's impression of the casting director, Katie's raucous cackle rang across the garden and Hamish's belly laugh barked the bass line.

When they had first met them, exhausted after an evening of the Nicholsons' jollity, a slightly shell-shocked Jay and Eliza had quietly agreed that when the couple laughed, they sounded like a donkey and a drunk Father Christmas. But as time had gone by, they had grown used to their loudness and become very attached to them, in particular Hamish.

The others chuckled and as he joined in, Eliza was relieved to see the gaunt, stretched look of Jay's usually handsome face lifting. He was already relaxing, as she had hoped. It looked like they were in for a fun evening. He always cheered up in Francesca's company.

"So, what was the audition for?"

Upping the tone, Eliza was aware that under her bravado, Francesca was becoming desperate for some acting work, not just for the money but also and maybe more for reputation.

"Oh, just a part in a fucking fringe play – probably rubbish anyway..." She did her usual performance of seeming unconcerned.

"Bad luck missing it though."

"Own fault – silly fool that I am. Thought Thursday was the twentieth when it was actually fucking Wednesday. Other way round I could have bedded down with an old friend, of which I have a few in the great metrop," she arched the eyebrows, "but 'twas not to be, 'twas not to fucking be."

In a gesture of sympathy, Eliza reached across under the table to pat her pal's knee and brushed against another hand that was clearly Bob's. But he didn't remove it. Nor did he look faintly embarrassed. That was who Bob was. Untroubled by what people thought of him, a man subject to his own rules.

A piercing wail shattered the peaceful village scene and brought an abrupt end to the conversation. Siren blaring, an ambulance hurtled past the Old Cock garden, heading towards Sparepenny Lane.

Deafened again by the scream of two police cars following the ambulance, the friends were alarmed. Things like this didn't happen in Heronsford.

"Oh God, you don't think it's something to do with the Ryans, do you?" Hamish addressed the air. Bob fished his mobile phone out of his pocket.

"Or Rose," said Eliza, looking at Jay, who looked anxious.

"I'll call Patrick."

It rang with no reply.

"I think we should walk down there and see if it's anything to do with the Ryans or Rose," said Jay. Drained of colour, he gulped down his beer, twisted his legs round the end of the bench and stood up. Katie followed suit and pulled herself up from the table, becoming hopelessly entangled with Homer who was running around in circles. Eliza followed suit and Francesca downed her drink at speed. They all set off to fast walk the half a mile towards Sparepenny Lane. As they drew nearer and turned into the lane, they could see the ambulance and police cars.

Passing Rose's cottage, Eliza and Jay were particularly relieved to find nothing unusual. Rose Cooper cleaned (or "mucked them out" as Annie joked) and did a bit of cooking for both Eliza and Annie. Eliza loved Rose deeply, who had been a large part of her life since she could remember. When she had been young and her mother was working much of the time in London, Rose had been employed as a daily nanny from Monday to Friday.

Along the lane, a young policeman was cordoning off Sparepenny Place with blue and white tape wrapped around a tree and a road sign. One by one the group sat down below a sycamore tree on the verge of the lane opposite the gateway to the house. Loud cracking sounds in the branches above made some of them jump and all of them glance up to see a couple of crows extricate themselves from the tree and flap away. They landed on the roof of the shed that was Louise's dark room in the garden. There was no sign of Patrick, Louise or their daughter Sinead.

Artistic, talented, could-be-difficult, from the men's perspective, Louise was a very attractive woman. But the wives were wary of her unpredictable and flirtatious nature.

Francesca was the closest to her. She found it easier to forgive her for sometimes being crabby and at other times for being ostentatious and loud-mouthed. By the same token, she could be great fun.

Louise was a good photographer who would only use film and pre-digital cameras to take photos of landscapes, places and, rarely, people, taken from unusual, distant angles. There was sometimes a hint of surrealism, and always solitude, about them. It was a passion for her and when she wasn't photographing, she was developing prints in a studio in their garden that was divided into a dark room alongside a small space with a sofa and a sound system for when she felt the need to escape. Her work was quirky and clever, but the photos of desolate, lonely places did not encourage many to buy them. A few committed fans and occasional exhibitions in Cambridge encouraged Louise to keep going. The daughter of the owners of a large group of department stores, she had plenty of her own money so could afford to be an artist without the "impoverished" label.

Patrick ran Ryan's Antiques on Trumpington Street, the road that leads past the Fitzwilliam Museum to link up with King's Parade in the city centre of Cambridge. Due to his eye for fine pieces of furniture, works of art and objects, as well as a gift of the gab, he had done well.

The friends were all aware that the Ryans were far from experiencing marital bliss but knew that both of them adored their only child and would do anything rather than upset her. In other words, they were together for the sake of their daughter. The couple was careful to avoid rows or disagreements in front of their friends and they did not allow their lack of harmony to affect their day-to-day lives. That Louise suffered from bouts of depression was known, and her friends did what they could to help, although when the darkness descended on the unstable woman, she tended to shut herself away, and them out.

Although Louise was a devoted mother, she was in fact a bad one, either over-cosseting and pampering Sinead or getting angry and shouting at her.

If they had been asked, their friends in the village would have admitted that it was because of Patrick's great likeability that they had befriended the couple. They saw how Louise pushed all of Patrick's buttons in order to get a reaction from him and they were amazed by his tolerance that was almost saintly at times. He was much appreciated for being the grounded, stable father that he was to Sinead, who certainly needed his balanced hand to counteract the uneven behaviour of her mother.

The group sat in shocked silence. Then, holding Sinead's hand, Rose came out of Sparepenny Place and walked slowly towards them. Both woman and child were clearly in a state of shock. The child kept glancing back at the house in what looked like fear. In spite of the colour drained from her usually pink cheeks, Rose's expression and stocky body confirmed a steady strength and compassion that was the most useful thing Sinead could do with. The girl, eyes puffy from crying, looked white, miserable and terrified.

Eliza and Francesca got to their feet and moved towards them. Eliza gave Rose a hug and a questioning look, to which Rose subtly shook her head to imply, "not now".

Francesca wrapped her arms around Sinead. "Can we do anything?"

"Not for the minute. We're going back to my place for some tea." The firmness of Rose's tone clearly inferred questions were off limits.

The traumatised child started to sob again. Rose gripped her hand. Her eyes watery with tears, the kind woman clearly had the situation under as much control as she was able.

Eliza felt helpless, "Call me if you want."

"I shall."

Rose and Sinead walked slowly on. They turned up the little pathway through an immaculate front garden to Rose's door. Her staunch husband Chris opened it. Eliza and the others knew the child could not be in a more caring place, with people who would do all they could to help her through whatever had happened. Chris often helped out at the farm and was devoted to Annie B. He would fetch and chop her firewood, and do any heavy jobs that needed doing in her garden, often refusing pay.

Still at the side of the lane but by now on their feet, the group hovered soundlessly. Eliza and Francesca returned with the news that they knew nothing more. Each quiet in their own thoughts, the wordless group walked back to the village. Driving at a slower pace, the ambulance passed them on its way back to the Cambridge hospital. When they reached the pub, there were no hugs this time.

Managing murmured goodbyes, white-faced Hamish and Katie got into their Toyota and Bob, dismay replacing his usually optimistic face, into his Mercedes. The others watched them drive away. Eliza linked arms with Francesca who seemed diminished by anxiety, while Jay followed slowly, looking quite shell-shocked.

"You're not spending the night alone until we discover what the hell has happened. You're staying with us and that's an order," said Eliza.

"You are not," echoed Jay, and as an afterthought, "I mean you are s-spending the n-night with us." He was stammering as he had done during his childhood.

"Thank you, thank you." Francesca flushed with gratitude. Of all the women in their little group, Francesca and Louise were probably the closest. They encouraged one another to drink to excess and to take cocaine, not used by the rest of the group. Louise was a wild child who wrestled her internal demons by self-medicating. The attractive, small-framed woman was only five foot two and unable to hold large amounts of alcohol without becoming drunk. But she never allowed herself to do this in front of Sinead and made sure that when she did have a binge, the child did not know.

As they walked back to Manor Farm, an anxious look on her face, Francesca said,

"I have this feeling Louise has OD'd. I just hope that session she and I had on Monday didn't have something to do with this. We did tie on quite a few as well as rather a lot of the old white powder and I am now worried I shouldn't have encouraged her. Perhaps she is too fragile for all that stuff. If she turns out to be okay, I'm promising myself and you all that I shall not do that stuff with her anymore."

Eliza put her arm through Francesca's. "Don't worry. I'm sure it wasn't anything to do with you. Presuming she's been taken to hospital, once she's out, I have a feeling it will have been a wake-up call for her and that it will turn out to be the best thing that could have happened."

7

22 JUNE

E liza went through the kitchen door to the corridor that led to the children's sitting room. She opened the door and went in.

"Hi, you two. Sorry but we're back early. Everything okay?"

Juliet and her boyfriend were into a heavy snog on the sofa. They were wrapped round one another's bodies. Determined not to embarrass another member of her family this evening, she tried to look as though this was normal in her house. The couple hastily unravelled themselves to sit upright. They both looked red-faced.

"We're fine, Mum. Watching Enders."

"So it seems," Eliza laughed to make light of the matter, but this only served to embarrass them further.

The dreamy-looking – if incredibly dull – boyfriend was now sitting well away from Juliet. At her daughter's age, Eliza would have been crazy about a boy that looked like him.

"Won't interrupt. Have you eaten?"

"Yes, thanks."

"Francesca's here and we're having supper in the kitchen."

"Okay. See you later."

They avoided eye contact both with Eliza and one another. When

Eliza returned to the kitchen, the unwashed-up evidence of their meal was in the sink.

"Well, it's either a bad accident, an OD, or, God forbid, a death. Whatever it is, it's horrible." When Francesca was serious about things or affected emotionally, she would stop her usual cursing. Eliza was relieved to see how sensitive Francesca could be.

"No point in conjecture," said the ever-practical Eliza. "And I'd rather not alarm the girls until we know what's happened, so mum's the word, okay?"

"This anxiety is making me feel sick," was her reply, but Francesca knew Eliza was right. For this evening, they should avoid the subject for all their sakes.

Jay crossed to the larder and reappeared with a bottle of red wine. He waved it in the air and the women nodded.

"I'll make some pasta." Eliza filled a large saucepan with water, salted it and put it on the hot plate of the old cream Aga that had been there since she was a child.

The kitchen was large and inviting with a mellow feel. Cheerful poppy-red walls, painted by Eliza, surrounded an irregular floor of old quarry tiles, some that had broken away at the edges or had split. The inglenook fireplace with an exposed brickwork surround of small, early English handmade bricks housed the ancient cream Aga and a once white butler's sink was still where it had been for more than half a century, although Annie had updated the taps twenty years ago. The house had surprisingly high ceilings for a half-timbered and brick farmhouse. This made the roughly hewn lime-washed beams on the ceilings not oppressive in the way that darkened ones can be.

The three sat at the long, old faded table eating their spaghetti Bolognese with little enthusiasm. Conversation loath to come to them.

Francesca in particular was unable to stop her imagination running riot while Jay stared with glum, teary brown eyes at the table.

But the drink kept flowing and once they had consumed a bottle, they began to realise that Eliza was right. That speculation would get them nowhere. She suggested a game of Scrabble to take their minds off it, but Jay, still looking shaken, said, "You two have a game. Sorry, but I think I'll turn in. Been a rotten evening."

When he'd left the room, Francesca said, "I've never seen Jay in such a state."

"Yes, I know. He's been in such a stress about the business, which has more or less hit the skids, and I think Bob showed him up this evening by paying for the drinks. Jay's such a proud man and now this awful business with the Ryans... it's all too much for him. The stutter's come back."

"Never heard him do that before."

"A long story."

"Tell?"

"Completely and utterly confidential, okay?"

Francesca mimed zipping her lips.

"Cross your heart and hope to die?"

"Of course!" The women linked their little fingers in a gesture of promise.

"Well... okay. Jay had a foul stepfather called Ralph, who he was terrified of as a kid. The bloody man hid it from the mother, but behind her back he mentally abused the poor little boy, constantly belittling him and tripping him up and threatening him with violence.

"Jay's older sister tried to protect him, but she just got threatened too.

"Their own dad had died when she was eight and Jay was only five. Their heartbroken mum had rebounded into marriage with this awful man. Jay developed a nervous stammer as a result. At least he was at boarding school when he was older, but by then the damage was done."

"Did his mother know what was going on?"

"Neither Jay nor his sister ever dared tell her because Ralph threatened to hurt their mother if they did. Then an incredible piece of luck saved Jay. One dark evening, Ralph's flash American car that he loved to race around in, skidded on a bend and he died hitting a tree. When the crash happened, Jay was thirteen. It turned out that one of the car's tyres had a puncture. Jay's wish had come true. Liberated by Ralph's death, he was at last able to tell his mother, who was mortified to learn how the horrible man had tormented her beloved son. She got him the best possible help for the stammer. He conquered it well, but it still returns when he is especially overtired, tense or emotional."

"So the stepfather was a penis with a penis extension car," murmured Francesca. "Poor Jay."

They discussed the Armstrongs' problems for a while and Eliza was grateful to unburden as Francesca was an excellent person to talk to about such things. Good at understanding how emotions can disturb and upset people, and at being sympathetic and helpful to them. This was one of the reasons Francesca was such a friend to Louise. Louise swung from being highly capable, driven, full of ideas and a thoroughly cheerful, fun person to be with to a badly depressed person, sometimes to the point where it almost crippled her. But she had been on medication for this for the past couple of years and it really did at last seem to be helping her temperament maintain a steadier balance.

Eliza was always surprised when the usually frivolous "party girl" Francesca became a serious down-to-earth friend. More surprising still was that, in such situations, she drank much less than usual. Being the counsellor suited her. This side rarely made an appearance and it made Eliza like her even more. It also explained why the woman was such a good actress. She could touch people's hearts because she understood the depths of their souls.

For a short time, the girls played a half-hearted game of Scrabble until giving up. By 10.30pm, the excess apprehension had tired them, and they too were grateful to call it an early night.

Having shown Francesca where the bathroom was, Eliza took her to the larger of the two spare bedrooms, turned down her bed and opened the window. She made to kiss her goodnight but instead gave her a big hug, saying, "Please try not to worry about it tonight, Francesca. There'll be enough time for—"

A powerful screech cut through the air. Francesca jumped. "What the fuck was that?"

Eliza patted her back. "Only the resident barn owl. Don't fret, darling, try to get some sleep." She hugged the unsettled woman again. "Happy dreams. Goodnight."

As she left the room, she silently told herself off for the second time that day for not having been careful enough with her words. How could Francesca be likely to have happy dreams in view of the evening's events?

Eliza was right. Her friend's dreams were not happy and neither did she have a good night. Nor, come to that, did Jay.

8

23 JUNE

Both Hamish and Katie were attempting, but failing, to neglect hangovers the following morning. Hamish was up by about eight thirty, allowing Katie to stay in bed a while longer. He made the children breakfast. A dependable chap, she knew he would make a smooth job of cooking for the tribe. A family that tended towards regimen, the Nicholsons always had weekend breakfasts of eggs, bacon, toast, tomatoes, mushrooms and spinach.

Like Jay, Eliza and Francesca, they had gone home to their house, eaten something and sat up drinking round their kitchen table, but unlike the others, they had drunk at least a bottle of red each.

Katie had wanted to stay up and discuss what might have happened at the Ryans' house but Hamish had not. That was unlike him in some ways, but then she had noticed that he wasn't quite himself lately. He didn't seem to want to sit up till late like they used to, and was prone to going to bed early these days. It had flitted across Katie's mind that he might have some sort of illness, but she knew that that was not really it. There was something else. *Probably worried about work,* she told herself, but a niggle remained in her mind. Had Hamish's love for the ladies or, worse, a lady, resurfaced? There was something going on, she was sure, just not about what it was.

Not ready to go to bed, she had stayed up to drink some more red wine, but before Hamish went up, they had agreed that as soon as the time was decent in the morning, Hamish would ring Jay to ask if there was any news. The Armstrongs might have spoken to Rose by then.

Rubbing half open, gungy blue eyes, Katie got up at about ten o'clock. With no need for a dressing gown in the heat that was already building up in the house, she almost tripped over a pair of sandals and scattered pile of clothes as her soft, chubby body stumbled towards the bathroom. Untidy by nature, Katie avoided housework as much as possible and was always behind with the washing and ironing.

The house was fairly chaotic, but Hamish, who might have minded once, had long since stopped allowing it to irritate him, apart from the occasions when he couldn't find any clean pants or milk in the fridge. He did his best to help in the house and it was not unusual to see him hoover, wash-up, tidy up, wash and iron.

Katie was hugely relieved that it was a weekend with no school. But then she realised that in fact it might have been better if they had been off to school. It would be easier to process whatever was in store regarding the Ryans without the children around the place.

Dreading what the day might bring, Katie threw on a sleeveless cotton top and shorts and went downstairs. The house was quiet. She found her children lounging in what was still known as the playroom but that now contained a large sofa, a homework table and chairs and a television in place of the earlier mess of toys.

She attempted to sound bright. "Morning, you two."

"Morning," they spoke in unison without looking up from their iPads.

"Any idea where Dad is?"

"Took Homer out," muttered Melissa.

"Thanks. How long ago?"

"Five minutes?" She still didn't even glance up at her mother.

Johnny said nothing. He just seemed irritated by his mother's interruption.

Katie went through the kitchen to the open French windows and stepped out into the garden. Cooler than yesterday, it was still sunny and warm. She scanned the fields beyond before spotting Hamish behind the big ash tree at the edge of the half acre site. He was talking on his mobile and looked terribly sad. She walked quietly over to his side. As she reached him, he hung up and changed his expression.

"Who?"

"Eliza," he replied. She saw he had been crying.

"And?"

"It's very bad news. Let's go and sit down." He led her by the hand to a wooden bench silvered by age.

"What's happened?"

He put a large muscly arm around her shoulders and squeezed her as though this might somehow take away from the pain of the situation.

"It's Louise."

"What's happened?"

"She, she... apparently..."

Katie looked at him. "She what?"

"She drowned herself."

Her voice was high. "Drowned? Herself? You mean she's dead? But she can't be!"

"She is, the poor woman. She is."

"Oh my God! I don't believe it."

She then asked the questions everyone always asks when somebody dies. "How? Where?"

"In their pool," his voice cracked.

"Their pool? But how could that possibly be? It's not possible, surely?"

"I know, that's what I thought."

"But, but..." The enormity of the news began to seep in.

Hamish dropped his head and looked at his trainers.

There was a long silence during which they both stared at the ground, trying to make sense of the news.

"But surely you can't drown yourself? I mean how? And surely... I mean, surely you'd stop yourself?"

"She couldn't swim, remember? I don't know any more. The ghastly facts are that she is dead and it's horrible and tragic."

"What can we do to help?"

"Jay says Rose has Sinead for the moment and that Louise's parents have already arrived. Patrick's are on their way but they're in the middle of Ireland so that will take time."

"And is Patrick at home?"

"He's going to spend tonight with the Armstrongs."

"We could have Sinead for a while."

"We could. I think Melissa would be fine, but given his current state of mind, do you honestly think Johnny would be okay with her?"

"Probably not. What an absolute nightmare this is."

"Nightmare," echoed Hamish.

At breakfast with Stella on Saturday morning, Bob McKenzie told the shocked young woman (whose cold had mysteriously gone) of the previous evening's events. Sitting at the long walnut marquetry table that could be extended to seat sixteen, the daily newspaper open before him, he pulled his mobile from his trouser pocket and called Jay.

Bob never beat about a bush. "Jay, morning. Any news re the Ryans?"

In a silk brocade white and silver knee-length kaftan, Stella sat quietly at her place at the table under a large expensive British abstract painting Bob had been encouraged by Patrick to buy. She watched her husband intently. He looked sad and worried.

"Okay, well give us a ring when you hear anything. Don't feel I should call Patrick today."

He rang off and looked at Stella across the table. "You're looking particularly beautiful today, my angel. White suits you. You should wear it more often. And I like your hair that way, my pretty girl."

"Thank you, darling. Happy you like."

Stella was much younger than the majority of women in Heronsford, and with no children to keep her busy, she must have been terribly bored. She was apparently happy keeping in shape in their gym, shopping in London's Sloane Street and Bond Street to spend extortionate sums on clothes and hairstyles, encouraged by Bob who liked her "looking her best".

The housekeeper made sure the manor was always immaculate and full of flowers arranged by Stella. The place was furnished with a mix of some wonderful and some over-embellished, gilded rococo antiques, as well as a few of the more classical pieces that Patrick had found for them. Bob revelled in throwing large extravagant parties where caterers provided amazing food.

There was, therefore, little for Stella to do except walk Fritz, the German shepherd, of which Eliza and Katie could tell she was actually afraid. On these walks, she would carry her beloved Chihuahua, Baby, the one thing she had in this foreign place that was her own.

An hour later, in his office in the house where he dealt with estate matters, Bob got a call on his mobile. "Bloody hell! Oh no! Jesus Christ! However did it happen?"

He listened to the short reply then murmured, "Yes, the poor guy. Poor kid. What an awful thing. How the hell?"

A pause and then, "Of course, of course. Anything Stella and I can do? Anything at all?"

A few more words then, "Okay then, well bye for now and don't forget, let me know if there's anything... thanks for letting us know."

He put his mobile back in his pocket and went to look for Stella, who was arranging a huge vase of flowers from the floral greenhouse.

"Stop that, angel. Sit down."

Stella laid a spray of blue delphiniums, eucalyptus leaves and white roses on a round Napoleonic table. She sat down on a red and gold silk damask gilded sofa raised on gilt legs. She crossed her own long elegant ones and shifted in her seat. It was obvious something dreadful had happened. Her husband looked shocked, upset and angry. She felt slightly sick.

Another pause then Bob said, "I have some very bad news. Poor Louise is dead. She drowned in their swimming pool. A terrible thing and a bloody shame. Can't think how it could happen. All very odd."

He leant forward and gripped the side of the table. He was obviously upset.

"Oh, how dreadful! But why? Why? I didn't know they had a pool." Stella looked horrified "That poor child. Such a lovely girl. This is so sad." She began to cry.

"I know, I know. I just hope there wasn't foul play behind this. I mean, it's just so odd. She'd seemed pretty happy lately. If so, what sort of fiend could do that to such a pretty little darling? Angel, now listen, while it's very sad, I don't want you worrying your lovely young head over it. Their families and closest friends will help. I've said we'll do all we can. Our turn will come later."

Typical of Bob to worry more about his wife than anyone else. He took her hand and squeezed it hard. "Don't cry, my sweetheart, don't cry. I don't want a sad girl in the house. Don't I do enough to make you happy, angel?"

"Of course you do, darling. Sorry," said Stella.

Fortunately, Francesca had not yet appeared that morning and was presumed to be sleeping after a bad night. At some time around 10.30am on Saturday morning, so that Juliet who was sitting in the kitchen on her iPad didn't overhear, their mother took her mobile upstairs to her bedroom and rang Rose.

From the cryptic way the woman spoke, it was obvious that Sinead was still with her and listening in the background. Via yes-no answers, Eliza was able to glean that Louise was dead. She couldn't ascertain how it had happened or why, but was able to establish that Louise's parents were with Patrick at Sparepenny Place.

When she had rung off, she walked along the landing to Francesca's door and quietly rapped. She heard a muffled response, opened it and went in.

In a mess of bedclothes half fallen on the floor, a sheet just covering her, Francesca was lying in her bra and briefs. She patted the bed and Eliza sat down. Struggling to maintain some decency and to sit up, she ran her fingers through dishevelled black hair.

"Cup of tea?" suggested Eliza brightly.

"Ooh, yes please." Francesca looked at her large, voguish watch. "Christ! Sorry, I'm still in bed. Horrible night. Any news?"

But Eliza was out of the door and running downstairs to get the tea. She needed Francesca compos mentis before breaking the news, but decided the bedroom was the best place to do it, with no-one else around. She made a cup and took it up to Francesca, ready to give her awful tidings.

Once Francesca had absorbed the meaning of the terrible information and cried loudly, she found her clothes, temporarily ceased weeping and descended to the kitchen to join Eliza and Juliet. Eliza was so glad Holly wasn't there.

The shrill sound of the landline startled them. Eliza answered. It was Patrick. He sounded extremely shaky and his long-forgotten Irish accent had returned. Voice breaking, he slowly managed to tell her about the tragedy at his house.

She pressed the phone to her ear and took it into the garden, out of earshot of Francesca and Juliet. With occasional pauses when he found it hard to continue, Patrick said he had been in his antique shop when the school had rung to say Louise had not appeared to collect Sinead and that they could not contact her. He received no replies to his phone calls so he had locked up the shop and raced to Heronsford School to collect his daughter.

There was no sign of Louise when they had got home. He had reassured Sinead that she would soon turn up (though sensing something bad had happened), and put her favourite DVD on the television, gave her a bag of crisps, some biscuits and a drink and settled her down on the sofa.

He had then looked everywhere in the house, meeting with an eerie silence. The next place he had checked was the garden. Here he had found Louise in her clothes, face down at the bottom of the pool.

He had dragged her body to the surface and somehow got her out. He had called the ambulance on his mobile and with the help of the 999 operator, had followed instructions while trying to resuscitate Louise but she had been gone for some time. It was too late.

The ambulance had come and... here Eliza saved him from

needing to say more. On with her practical hat, she must deal with the here and the now.

"Words fail me, Patrick. It's the most terrible, horrible thing and I just cannot believe you're having to deal with something so awful." There, she had said it, and now to the matters in hand. "We know Sinead is with Rose, and would love to have her here for as long as it takes if that would help. Holly and she can do things to keep her busy, and they get on very well."

"She couldn't swim, she couldn't swim! I just can't understand why she chose to die in the pool. Oh, mother of God, she... she looked so weird."

"Is anyone there with you? Can we help?"

"Louise's parents arrived late last night and are staying here. They have gone to see Sinead and take her home with them for a while. I'm just... I just... I don't know..."

"Patrick, we will do whatever we can to help. What about you? If you would like to stay too, we would be so pleased to help. In fact, we would be so happy to have either or both of you. Just call whenever you want. We're around and are not going anywhere. Sort out with the grandparents what's best for you and Sinead."

Low sobs came from the phone.

"The police are everywhere. They're all over the house and garden. I... I have to go..."

"We're here," was all Eliza could think to say before replacing the phone in its cradle. The shock then hit. Her heart hurt.

The phone went again. It was Hamish. Choking over the words, she told him that Louise was dead. Unable to say more, she kept the phone call short.

She then sought out Jay who was in the office. She broke the news. He looked so desperately sad. Then he said, "I had the feeling when I saw the police there yesterday. I thought it was Louise. That poor darling, she was so fragile. All that tough girl can do stuff was a front. Poor, poor Louise."

Eliza said, "I know she had her ups and downs, but was sure she would never..."

When Jay cried, it gave her permission and for the first time, Eliza let go too. Surprised at the ease with which her husband shed tears, she realised that the same thing was happening to her. It was such a shocking way to die. Louise might not have been her best friend in the world: she had been too outspoken and formidable for Eliza's taste, but she had been fond of the woman, especially when she had showed her quieter side, when she had become much softer and more vulnerable. Though if truth was told, the kinder of the two by a long chalk was the gentle, soft-spoken Patrick, whom Eliza liked more.

She wanted Jay to give her a hug. She walked round to the side of his chair and put an arm round his shoulders. But he didn't respond; not even look up at her.

She withdrew her arm. What was happening to them? Why was Jay withdrawing from her? It wasn't her fault the company was in trouble, any more than it was his. And she hadn't considered laying any blame at his door. Or was blame the reason? Was it about something else? Was she putting too much on it, over-imagining again? She knew she had a strong imagination and told herself that he was just worried at the moment. Why wouldn't he be, after all? They used to talk about any problems and always managed to iron them out. But he had almost stopped communicating with her. As though he were avoiding her. She had never seen him like this, but then they'd never been through anything like this before.

Eliza left Jay without saying another word. She hesitated in the yard then changed direction towards her mum's house. She felt the need for someone who could give comfort. And if anyone could do that, it was Annie B. Just about everyone referred to Annie Berkeley as Annie B., the name her grandchildren had started calling her. The comforting familiarity of her nickname suited her well since both her character and her appearance had an inviting friendliness about them.

Eliza didn't bother to knock. She walked straight in to find Annie had just returned from her routine morning dog walk in Rooks Wood. She was sitting in her favourite armchair reading the paper.

"The most terrible thing has happened."

Annie got up and came over to Eliza, who was white-faced and tearful. With her arms outstretched, she said, "Whatever is it, darling?"

"Louise has drowned herself in their pool."

If that's what her child said, then that's what had happened, so Annie saw no point in repeating the phrase in question form. In her years as a barrister, she had come across some very horrible things and just about nothing surprised her any more. She hugged her child tight. "How just dreadful. Oh darling, I am so sorry. A depressive, wasn't she?"

"Well, she was certainly an up-and-down sort of person and used to have some bad bouts of lows, but since she'd been on medication, she had seemed a lot better. Why do you ask?"

"I just wondered whether she may have overdosed and then got into the pool." She paused. "Those two weren't happy, were they?"

Eliza wondered how and why her mother had picked up on such a thing. She had, after all, only met them perhaps three times at Sunday lunch at the farm, at which Annie was a permanent fixture. "You're very perceptive, Mum. What's so, so odd about this is that she couldn't swim and was quite afraid of the water. It was one of her neuroses–"

Annie interrupted her, "Then how ever did she manage it?"

"Heavens knows why she decided to do it in the pool, and I cannot imagine for the life of me how she did it. There are many better ways to commit suicide. And she loved Sinead, and although she and Patrick were no longer in love, she didn't hate him and would have been horrified to think of the child or Patrick finding her there."

"It's a very strange way to die."

"And you'd think her survival instinct would kick in and she would scrabble her way out without actually drowning."

"You would. Do we know whether she left a note?"

"Not as far as I know."

Eliza held onto her mother. They stood quietly while Eliza cried some more. Then, taking her hand, her mother led her to the sofa and sat down beside her. She said, "Have the children been told?"

"Not yet. I have to break it to them. Francesca's staying and she was such a close friend of Louise's. I've got to tell the children, and it's possible Patrick may come as I've offered to have him tonight. Luckily Holly had a sleepover with the Kendalls last night." Her long thin hands covered her face. "I've got to pick her up later and will have to tell her then. She's a good friend of Sinead's, so will be very upset."

"How old is Sinead?"

"They'll both be twelve in November. They're very much kindred spirits so I think Holly will be a great help to the poor little thing."

"I'll collect Holly for you," said Annie. "You've more than enough on your plate. I'll tell her what's happened and bring her back here for a little while until she's taken it in. What time does she need collecting?"

"Oh, thank you, Mum. Er, we said about five o'clock-ish, I think."

"Where's Jay? Being any help?" There was no wool to be pulled over Annie's eyes.

"He's not in a good way, Mum. His stutter has started to come back. This business with poor Louise seems to have been the last straw. He's in bits."

"A worried one, that man." Jay's recent inability to be strong for his family had seriously annoyed Annie, but she had a forgiving heart and had experienced how helpless some men could be in times of acute pressure. There was enough of an actress in the old barrister to make sure Eliza didn't see her feelings. "He's a very sensitive man, Eliza. One of the reasons you love him." She paused. "Any hope he could get away for a week or so?"

"I hope he will go on Bob's annual fishing thing in Scotland. But that's not until September."

"How about suggesting he visits his sister in Wales for a few days, and soon? That might help him get some perspective on all this."

"I hadn't thought of that. Good idea." She glanced at her watch, "I'd better go. God, I'm dreading today."

"Of course. The children mustn't know how. Not yet, anyhow. Holly might mention it to Sinead and we don't know what she's been told."

"Lunch tomorrow may be on hold, Mum. It depends on what Patrick wants to do."

"Actually, Pam has invited me for lunch and chess. I was going to tell you I wouldn't make it this week." She put an arm round her shoulders and pulled her daughter toward her. "Chin up, my brave girl."

When Eliza had left, Annie thought about what she had heard. So, Louise couldn't swim. Annie found it hard to believe that she would choose that way to kill herself. She thought of Virginia Woolf's tragic suicide. But that poor woman had made sure to end her life by putting heavy stones in her pockets. She recalled Louise's seductive behaviour where the men were concerned, and she wondered.

Putting the subject out of her mind, Annie decided that once things had settled a bit, she would suggest a game of chess with Jay. He liked playing when he found time and it might help relax him. She pondered whether she could gently try to persuade him to open up to her about his worries while they were playing. Talking it through would be so good for him. Annie could read the tension in his face and knew he was his own worst enemy in that sense. Jay had always been someone who kept his thoughts to himself and although Eliza was the closest anyone had ever come to him, Annie understood that it was terribly difficult for him to talk to his wife about his serious concerns when she was also his business partner.

On the other hand, she was his mother-in-law. She and Jay were good friends who loved one another but she was who she was, which could make it hard for him to talk to her about the business. She knew he had found the gift of Manor Farm difficult to handle. His pride had found it challenging to accept that his in-laws had given him a leg up when he would have preferred to pay for the family home himself. It would have been churlish for him to refuse to live there, especially as Eliza loved the place so. And now he had become used to it, he had grown to love the farm too, seduced by the setting and the charm of the old place. Like a duck to water, Jay had taken to looking after the land, mending fences, repairing outbuildings when they needed it and ensuring the ditches were cleared.

Annie knew his major concern was the prospect of not being able to afford to live there anymore, and could see what a difficult position he found himself in. She also understood that his pride would never get over it should the business become bankrupt. He would never live it down. She felt terribly sorry for him and did so wish she could help. But her wise head told her she had done enough for them and that he would never be able to accept further help from her. She'd suggest a game of chess with him and see what came of it.

Annie's friends knew her as a warm person with a sharp intelligence that shone from a square face with a mouth that turned slightly upward at the corners, giving her the appearance that life amused her, which in many respects it did. She thought of herself as a woman of the people as she had indeed been, when a successful defence barrister. A plucky person, she had taken on cases others wouldn't touch and had done well for many whom, on account of their lack of funds and education, might otherwise have languished in prison for much longer than they should. She had focused her energy on something that had real meaning for her, especially as, in her view, her work helped create a balance and equality in a world that was full of social injustice and inequality. Juggling work and life had become something of an issue. The job had demanded she spend much time in the London courts, most often the Old Bailey.

Her adored husband, a tall, lanky, nice-looking man, had been soft, loving and funny. Some might call him lazy or spoilt: his only jobs had been to help care for Eliza and paint pictures. He'd been taught at the Slade School of Art and was a respected East Anglian artist who held regular local exhibitions and who had been employed by many local landowners with large houses to paint them in a flattering light. He had painted for his living all his life. He had inherited money from his father that had helped him choose what Eliza had later come to see was an extremely easy life. This small inheritance had soon been spent and while his wife had worked hard, Robin had pottered about at home, painting for part of every day. He had not helped around the home much and when he did, had bungled attempts to change light bulbs, mend fuses, et cetera. He had been an impractical man, and Annie had realised it was easier to do it herself or get someone in to do it.

Eliza had an innate desire to lead a similar life to her father, but as she had become a teenager, she had seen how incompetent and ineffectual her adored father really was, and had fought that feeling in herself. She knew now that her mother, often begrudged by the young girl for her absence, was actually the one who had kept them all from going under. In her adult years, Eliza sometimes wondered how her mother had tolerated the situation, but however irritable Annie may have become with her amiable, insouciant husband, she knew she had loved him.

Eventually, Annie had decided that in order to save her marriage she would need to pull back on the number of cases she took on. When she had done this, spending more time at home had frustrated this vibrant woman, especially since her husband had spent much of the time on his own painting landscapes. Sometimes she had wondered why she had bothered, but her child had been the constant reminder that she had done the right thing.

She looked across the flat grass field that was divided from her garden by a barbed wire fence. Eeyore had kept company with the family ponies for many years and grazed lazily beside old Jock. The pony had been Eliza's last before she had decided art, along with two-legged boys, held more appeal than Jock.

To separate the garden from the countryside beyond, when Annie had moved into the barn, she could have had a high or low hedge planted or any kind of fence from picket to feather board. To the surprise of her architect, she had insisted the edge of her land stayed as it always had been. Ever since she had been at Manor Farm, she had appreciated the broad, open view that culminated in Rook's Wood, the long sweep of woodland that belonged to the farm and ran along the horizon. And she liked the authenticity of the barbed wire. That the landscape stretched westward was better still as Annie could sit in her sitting room or on her patio and watch the sunsets that were particularly striking in August and September.

In this hot weather, if she'd been younger, she would have hitched up her skirt, run past the animals and taken a dip in the river that curved round the far border of the field. She remembered the races she used to have with Robin to reach it first. Very like her father, their child, tall, artistic, dreamy and gentle-natured, reminded her of him every time she saw her. Resolutely unsentimental, Annie quickly brought herself back to the present and remembered the dwindling watershed. The river that curled around the house and land in an arc had once run full and free flowing. It had decreased in depth and sometimes became clogged with plants and needed dredging every so often. It was currently overgrown with reeds and other water plants, for the dry weather had turned it into little more than a rivulet.

Eliza dragged her feet when walking back to the house. Now she had to break it to Juliet. As she went, she was surprised when Jay strode across the yard from the office, caught up with her, put an arm round her shoulders and murmured, "Sorry to have been such a flake earlier."

Eliza felt a flood of relief wash over her that she would not have to deal with this dreadful event single-handed. Her shaken faith in Jay felt almost ready to be restored.

Francesca had great trouble digesting the fact that her friend had gone, let alone so suddenly.

"When the poor little darling was only six years old," said Francesca, "she was swimming in the sea close to the beach when a vicious ten-foot wave came out of nowhere, picked up her little body and swept her out to sea. She was saved by her father but had never forgotten the helpless feeling of being like a piece of flotsam, and the terror. Since then no amount of endeavour by her parents had persuaded her to learn to swim and she had been afraid of water ever since. In spite of this, determined that her daughter wouldn't be hampered by the same phobia, Patrick and she had built a swimming pool for Sinead, who is now an accomplished swimmer."

Listening to this, the others teared up again.

"Such a tragic waste," said Jay.

"So terribly young," said Eliza.

Francesca couldn't stop thinking about her friend's drowning and how an idea like that could have taken hold of her and, more to the point, why? The last time she had seen her at their drinking session, Louise had seemed upbeat and, after all, she had arranged to meet them all in the pub that evening. She had a lover, so why end it now? Anxious questions pounded Francesca's brain.

Sinead travelled back with her grandparents to their home in Cheshire. The idea of staying in their house alone was as abhorrent to Patrick as it had been for his daughter. He gratefully took up Eliza's offer to stay the night. Francesca stayed on as well. She had offered to leave but, on the principle that many hands might help to make lighter work of such a difficult time, Eliza had insisted she stayed for at least one more night.

Jay made it plain that the last thing he felt they needed was to have Patrick to stay. "What about the children, Eliza?" he muttered when he cornered her in the kitchen. "Doesn't he have some friends or family? They'd be better placed to deal with him."

Eliza was relieved they were talking, and that, for once in this difficult time, she agreed with him. "I didn't think he'd take us up. What can I do? I can't... it's too late now. Sorry, darling."

"Oh well. If it helps the poor guy out..." said Jay.

"It's only for a night. His parents are on their way over from Ireland and they'll be here in the morning. And there's that friend north of Cambridge who's going to have him for a bit. It's just that Patrick didn't want to drive when he was so exhausted."

The truth, though he hadn't told them, was that the police had insisted Patrick stayed in the village and at an address they knew, and that he must return to his house by 8.30am the following morning. He was still considered a prime suspect while they searched for clues.

It was after six by the time Patrick appeared and it was a difficult evening for them all. To spare them, Eliza gave the girls meals on trays in the playroom where they could watch television.

Jay made the excuse of feeling unwell and went to bed as early as possible, leaving the women and Patrick at the kitchen table. Francesca and Eliza soon discovered that trying to help someone deal with a sudden death, especially such a tragic one, was very hard.

But later, they were glad they had because the evening had been good for Patrick, who talked and talked and talked. The women were taken aback by his feelings of disbelief, anger, guilt, confusion, shock, horror and trauma that seemed to go beyond the "normal" emotions following a death. Of all the feelings he gave vent to, anger was by far the strongest. The unconditional willingness of the women to sit, listen, hold his hand and even hug him when he cried, was the first step on his long road ahead of living with death's residue.

They finally headed for bed at about two in the morning. Francesca went back to the bedroom she had stayed in the previous night and Patrick was given the other, smaller spare room. They fell into their beds so exhausted by emotion that even Patrick managed to sleep.

On Saturday, the local paper announced the news on its front page.

THE CAMBRIDGE NEWS

FEMALE PHOTOGRAPHER DROWNED IN SWIMMING POOL

Yesterday, Mrs Louise Ryan was found drowned in the family swimming pool at her home in Heronsford.

The tragedy happened at Sparepenny Place, a large property on the outskirts of the village. The sprawling home has a swimming pool in its rear garden surrounded by stone paving. The body lay undiscovered for several hours before Mrs Ryan's husband, Patrick, owner of Ryan's antique shop in Cambridge, returned to the property after spending the day in his shop on King's Parade. Mr Ryan called the emergency services and officers from Cambridge attended the scene as well as paramedics who pronounced his wife dead at the scene. It is not known how Mrs Ryan came to be in the water or how the death occurred since, as far as is known, no-one was present when she died. There will be a coroner's report and an inquest. At present, the death is being treated as suspicious.

LATE JUNE TO LATE JULY

The death of Louise Ryan had been estimated at somewhere between twelve noon and 2pm on 22 June 2018.

The forensic pathologist had been called to the scene where she had thoroughly examined the body. The police now needed to prove that Patrick or someone else had or had not murdered Louise who had been the daughter of rich parents and well off in her own right. The investigation showed her husband stood to inherit her money as well as a sizeable life insurance.

When the pathologist later examined the body in her laboratory, she found traces of white cotton fibre in the woman's mouth that suggested something had been stuffed into it either by herself or somebody else. There were no signs that the fabric had been forced into the mouth, which corroborated the suicide theory. But where was whatever it was? The pathologist felt uncomfortable about the detail and had the hunch that the fibres belonged to a handkerchief. But there was no evidence of bruising or marks on the body to suggest foul play.

There were quite a number of dark lividity marks caused after death by the husband grabbing the body and pulling it out of the pool, then attempting resuscitation.

Perhaps the woman, who she understood couldn't swim, had put it in her own mouth to make it hard to breathe. It would be, she supposed, quite an ingenious way to die.

The big question for the police was: why wasn't it still in the dead woman's mouth or in the pool? Had someone removed it before the police had arrived? If so, who?

Alerted by the pathologist, Cambridgeshire Constabulary searched the house and garden for the missing piece of cotton, but with no luck.

They checked out Patrick's alibi that he was in his shop. Fortunately for him, he had sold a table that had to be delivered to the customer. The police traced and visited the customer in question, who corroborated Patrick's story that he was definitely in the shop between 12.35 and 12.50, the time the buyer had been there deliberating about the table before purchasing it, then making arrangements for its delivery.

Patrick's car had been in the Trumpington Park and Ride car park, so he would have had to catch a bus (or a taxi) there, drive to Herons-ford, do the deed, and drive (and bus) back to his shop. It was impossible that he could have driven home in the window of time in which Louise had lost her life.

Was it someone Louise had invited in? But Fred Newman, who lived in a council house next door to Rose's, had been gardening in his front garden most of the morning. In his broad East Anglian accent, he told the officer interviewing him, "None walked by, that I'm certain and I'd have noticed a car. That's a dead-end to Sparepenny Place so there's few cars go by, 'cepting theirs."

"Any bikes?"

He shook his head. "No, no bicycles."

"Got any witnesses that you were in your garden?"

"Rose was in hers and we was chatting over the hedge. She didn't see nuthin' neither."

The detectives concluded that if Louise had invited someone in, they could not have come by the front way.

The police checked the road that passed the back of the Ryan's garden but there were no houses along there. They noted that this would be a good way for any intruder to avoid being seen and checked the wooden padlocked gate that led from the road down a little path through trees to the garden near the dark room. But there was nothing to suggest anyone had forced the gate or even climbed it. It was very dry weather so any hope of finding footprints was a no go. There was nothing else either; no broken undergrowth, no tell-tale signs of breaking and entering to go on.

Doctor Gordon confirmed prescriptions for antidepressants and told them about Louise's problems with mood swings. The autopsy revealed that she had recently consumed antidepressants and a large amount of alcohol.

The villagers held their own opinions and most people decided the death had been no accident. Suspicion hung in the air.

Patrick arranged with Heronsford School for Sinead to have compassionate leave until the end of term. She stayed with Louise's parents for a few days and then went with Patrick's parents, who took her to Ireland for a couple of weeks where they also visited Sinead's aunt, uncles and cousins.

Louise's burial could not go ahead until the inquest had taken place. It took about a month before an open verdict was reached. There was insufficient evidence to support any other verdict. The coroner recorded her drowning as death by misadventure.

While Sinead was away, Patrick spent as many nights as he could staying with friends. He wanted to avoid his home. But he had to stay locally until the inquest was over and Louise's body was finally released.

The day of the funeral started as a heavy one, the sky chalk grey, the air stuffy, the feeling oppressive.

Louise had been a committed Humanist and Patrick tried hard to make the service as palatable as possible for Sinead's sake. But in spite of the decorative flowers, crematoriums remain bleak modern places that do not demand the natural reverence people tend more towards in churches.

As a close friend of Louise's, Francesca gave a both moving and funny eulogy that helped to lift the mood, but there was no getting away from the fact that a young mother aged thirty-six had died a tragic death and left a heartbroken child behind her. It was a mournful affair.

The wake was held in the village hall because Patrick couldn't face having people back to the place where Louise died. The friends tried to be as sensitive as possible and quietly hugged one another.

Annie watched the husbands present for signs of more than the normal grief everyone felt. It flitted across her mind that the death might have something to do with a sexual liaison. She had noticed Louise had been a "player" when it came to the men and that most of them had been quite captivated by the coquettish, pretty little woman.

The usually reserved Stella looked appropriately sad and seemed genuinely sorry for Patrick and Sinead. Bob, too, was quieter than normal. Patrick had made known his decision to sell the house as fast as possible and move Sinead to Cambridge.

Bob approached him. "Found you a buyer for your place – they've seen the brochure and they want it. What's more, I have got you the perfect house in Cambridge. Three bed, pretty garden, Victorian, near your shop and Sinead's school. It's empty and the vendors are keen to be rid soon as. McKenzie's will bridge you a loan until your place here is sold, so you can move to Cambridge quickly if that's what's wanted. Come see me on Monday morning and we'll get the ball rolling." He patted the astounded Patrick on the back as the widower choked out his gratitude.

"No problem, no problem, old boy. Best if you move on quickly, hey?"

"Yes indeed. I'll see you on Monday, and thanks so much, Bob," Patrick stumbled over the words.

Born in the early seventies, Bob had come from a working-class, low-income family in a small town to the south of Norwich. He had proved extremely bright and won a place in a grammar school. From there, his dream to become rich had taken him to Cambridge where opportunities proliferated. Too impatient to wait for money to come his way, by the age of eighteen he had sussed the real estate market as the easiest place to achieve his aspiration and started working as a junior estate agent.

The ambitious young man had borrowed the money from a friend for a deposit to buy a cheap, tired, grubby one-bedroom flat. A lick of paint, an updating of the bathroom and kitchen at little cost and he had sold it a year later for almost double what he paid. By the age of twenty-four, he had founded Robert McKenzie Estate Agents with the same school friend who put in a large sum of money to fund the business in its first year. A few years on, apparently the school friend had a eureka moment when he had decided to travel the world and had dropped out of the business to leave Bob the sole owner.

McKenzie's now had countless branches across the south east of England from Oxford to Cambridge to Chelmsford in what Bob called the Golden Triangle. McKenzie's could even hold its own against the grand regional estate agents with offices in London drawing in property owners looking to sell.

Bob ran this company with a ruthless, tough attitude and was known for a heartless approach to those who didn't come up to scratch. In the days when bosses could get away with such behaviour, Bob was renowned for sacking people for the slightest misdemeanour. Everyone who worked for him was a little scared of him and did their best to stay on his right side.

His background and family far behind him, Bob had got rid of his

Norfolk accent long since and adopted the ways and manners of the well off. This did not surprise anyone who knew him. Social status mattered greatly to Bob. He liked being "the squire" and enjoyed being part of a slightly younger local set that looked up to him and was impressed by his money. In his relationship with Stella, it was clear to everyone that while he adored her, it was on his terms and there was no doubt about who was the boss.

Some of their female friends with more age on their side than the inexperienced young Swede, were irritated by Stella's apparent obeisance to her husband and the way she sometimes seemed to fear him. They felt she should stand up for herself and one or two of them said as much to her. They, though, were not married to the man. Stella was.

The Armstrongs, the Nicholsons and Francesca stood in a miserable huddle, the toys from the toddler group that also used the hall on happier days, stacked incongruously behind them. Conversation stuck in their throats.

Bob sauntered over. "Now then, boys, time to get Scotland filled up. Palace is booked. You two are joining me as usual?" Bob loved his annual Scottish salmon fishing holiday that combined shooting, a thing he enjoyed even more. He took eight double bedrooms in Scone Palace in Perthshire, a nineteenth century gothic building that is nowadays a luxurious hotel for people willing to pay for the privilege of staying on the site of the original crowning place of Scottish monarchs. The wing Bob took included a private dining room and its own kitchen. He also hired a chef for the ten days that were an entirely masculine affair, no wives invited. The Palace is situated on the River Tay, the biggest salmon fishing river in Scotland. Deer were profuse for stalking and grouse on a moor for shooting were close by.

Hamish couldn't get the words out fast enough. "I'm on, I'm on, no question about it, Bob, and thanks as always for the invitation. Been looking forward to it all year..." he hesitated as he realised this sounded presumptuous, "...I mean, I was really hoping you'd ask again.

No better place I can think of for a good time. Yes, definitely count me in, and thanks again."

A look of mild panic appeared on Jay's face. "Really g-good of you to ask, Bob, but this year I'm really s-sorry to have to say I c-can't."

Irritation flickered across Bob's face. "What d'you mean, you can't? Why ever not?"

Eliza butted in, her words tumbling out. "It's a matter of cash flow, Bob. Not sure if you knew but things have gone a bit pear-shaped with the business at the moment. I believe Jay should go as I know how much he loved it before. It would do him so much good to forget about the company for a while. I'm certain we can cobble together the cost."

"No cobbling about it, I'll cover any costs, old boy. Now look, Jay, you're expected and you're coming." Bob flashed a fleshy grin.

Jay had seldom felt so humiliated. He cast a black look at his wife. If this had been discussed privately between the two men, it would not have felt so bad, but in front of the women and Hamish, it was such a loss of face.

Hamish felt almost as uncomfortable as Jay.

Eliza instantly regretted her interception. As well meant as it may have been, she should have kept her trap shut. *I could have discretely rung Bob another day,* she thought.

Jay stammered a grateful thank you but said he really couldn't accept.

"Can't accept? Can't accept? What sort of a line is that, Jay?" The grin gone, infuriation marked Bob's face. "No buts about it. I told you, you're coming. I'm paying and that, old lad, is final, okay?"

For Jay, this was just about the last straw. He liked Bob well enough and knew the man was generous, but this was patronising beyond anything.

Bob was apparently unaware of their increasing discomfort and carried on discussing the dates for the holiday.

As they were leaving, Bob quietly took hold of Jay's arm and moving away from the people, said, "Listen, Jay, I am aware that you and Eliza are in some financial difficulties and I want you to know that I am more than happy to help out. I would keep this entirely between us, of course. I can give you the amount you need to clear any debts or keep the ship afloat and you have no need to pay me back. I like you, Jay. I like you a lot and I want to help. If you need a few strings pulling in the buying departments of any of the shops you usually have stock in, I can get people leaned on, know what I mean? I have contacts." He winked.

Jay was so taken aback by what Bob had said that his stammer made him almost incomprehensible. *And such an inappropriate time to have said it,* he thought. But he managed to stutter, "Good Heavens, Bob. I don't know what to say."

"Aha yes, I can see that, old boy. Anyway, offer's there. Have a think about it. Let me know... soon."

Although it sounded purely altruistic, there was something Jay found almost menacing about the way Bob had approached and spoken to him. But then Jay's pride had dogged him all his life and was more than likely the reason behind his feeling.

Things slowly settled back nearer to normal in Heronsford. The group of friends naturally rallied round to help Patrick as much as they could and both Katie and Eliza often invited Sinead to play with their own children and to have "sleepovers", as much to bring her some joy as to give Patrick the occasional evening off.

Francesca did as much as she could to care for Sinead, even having her to stay for the odd night between her visits to her grandparents and making sure to keep her busy with trips to Cambridge and London. She wanted to give the child the feeling that she would always be around for her, appointing herself "honorary godmother" to underline the fact.

Having learnt from her childhood, watching in the kitchen of her parents' restaurant, she cooked delicious Italian meals for the child and tried to lift her spirits in any way she could.

Unaware of it she may have been, but Sinead was grateful for Francesca's warmth and ability to lift her out of the doldrums.

Two weeks later, sitting on a bench in his garden talking on his mobile, Patrick Ryan looked down to the covered pool that no-one had been near since Louise's death. A mixture of relief and sadness coloured his mood today. When Sinead came out of the back door to join him, he said a quick goodbye, pocketed his phone and smiled at his daughter.

"I have some good news for you," he said, patting the seat beside him.

Sinead cocked her head. He put an arm round her shoulder and gave her a squeeze.

"I've accepted an offer on the house. We should be out of here in a few weeks. And," hesitating to give weight to what followed, "I have had an offer accepted on the perfect house for us in Cambridge. We can move into it almost straightaway!"

Sinead gave the first proper smile he had seen since her mother's death. "Yippee!" she said. "When can I see it?"

"I thought you'd say that. And guess what, we have an appointment this afternoon."

Sinead hugged her father. "That's so cool."

"You said it." They high-fived.

That afternoon they drove to Cambridge, parked in the Grand Arcade and met the estate agent.

Later that evening when Sinead had gone to bed, Patrick sat up. The mood that had descended earlier now returned, sorrow becoming the main feeling. *Where had everything gone so terribly wrong?* he wondered. But he knew and he also knew that as far as their marriage had been concerned, he had done his best to keep it together. Louise's nature had been against them and he knew that had her death not intervened, they were headed for the rocks. He felt bad about everything, but it was too late now and all he could do was try to be the best possible parent for Sinead.

On the last Saturday of July, the annual Heronsford village fête was held in the gardens of the manor as by tradition it always had been. This was organised by a committee of the Friends of Heronsford Primary School that included Eliza, who had been a pupil.

Since Bob McKenzie had bought the manor, he had been keen to continue to allow the fête to take place in the garden. Eliza sometimes wondered if it gave him a kick to see the villagers impressed by the grandeur of the setting and benevolence of the powerful, magnanimous man who owned it. But she quickly followed this with a kinder thought: he did it because he wanted acceptance from the village. After all, he was happy to muck in at the pub with everyone else, so he could hardly be accused of snootiness.

Although the air was clearer than it had been, the heat was building once again and the sun hot enough to warm the bottles on the bottle stall. The best cake competition, in which Rose was often a contender, was held inside the small marquee so although icings made of butter, cream cheese and ganache become softer, they didn't altogether melt.

Wearing a scarlet sunhat that did her no favours since her face had turned a pinkish crimson in the hot weather, a famous local author of successful crime fiction opened the fête. She stood four-square in a frumpy, flowery dress, gave a short speech and an introduction to the pre-school infants who sang *The Wheels on the Bus*. This was followed by older schoolchildren singing and drumming on an array of different things including inverted saucepans, upside down buckets and cymbals. Accompanied by bells, tambourines and whistles, the ensemble played a medley of famous pop songs, generating good spirits in the crowds and putting smiles on people's faces.

By contrast (and avoided by most) a group of traditional English Morris Men performed late medieval ritual dances in the courtyard. They wore straw hats embellished with flowers and were dressed in white shirts and trousers with colourful criss-cross sashes, armbands, rosettes and bell pads on their shins. They wielded sticks and handker-chiefs as they stepped and skipped and jumped and stamped their formal dances to tunes played by a small man on the accordion.

In the gardens, there was a tombola, a raffle, a hoopla, a coconut shy, a competition for the best cake, a bottle stall, children's games like Grandma's footsteps, bat-the-rat, get the ball through the croquet hoop and lucky dip.

Stella would be helping to run the best cake competition – but that came later. So she drifted around looking gorgeous in high wedged bright blue sandals and a long sheer flowing turquoise, blue and green cover-up that barely did its job over a décolleté pale blue strappy top and matching shorts. Her tanned, toned legs seem to go on forever and there wasn't a man present who could stop himself ogling.

Never to be upstaged, Francesca wore a hot pink belted dress that showed off her curves to the maximum, high-soled beige trainers and, topping the outfit, a large pink hat with a rim as curvaceous as the rest of her. While the local men lusted after Stella, they also appreciated Francesca's obvious delight in her own femininity and her natural flamboyance.

Early on she had found the bar tent and, wine glass in hand, took part in all the games with great enthusiasm. Her role at the fête would come later when an hour and a half before the finish she was to paint faces for the younger children, her theatrical training at stage make-up standing her in good stead.

Jay should have looked handsome in his blue T-shirt and long navy shorts, while he manned the bat-a-rat stall, but his demeanour prevented it. The tension in his face still showed and his good looks that had vanished due to the strain he was under, had not returned.

Although they had no orders yet, the buyers for a famous chain department store were showing interest in the newly-released Eliza Berkeley Designs trade catalogue, in particular Fruit 'N' Veg. Another large London shop was also talking of ordering. The factory workers had been laid off and put on half pay while Jay had struggled to keep the business afloat.

But manning the bat-a-rat stall took his mind off things. The player stood ready with the rubber bat while he dropped the rat (actually an old fluffy squirrel found in the Armstrong children's toy box) down a vertical plastic tube. It required just enough of his concentration that it was difficult to dwell on his business worries.

Katie ran the tombola and Hamish was on the coconut shy. Bob was running an adult-only clay pigeon shooting competition in a paddock beyond the main garden.

In a smaller field beside the paddock, Eliza led Jock the pony to and fro with small children riding on his back. After an hour and a quarter she stopped as she felt the old pony was getting too hot and tired. Quietly relieved, she led him away from the fête and back along the lanes to Manor Farm.

Never one for large group activities and crowds, Eliza hadn't enjoyed her afternoon any more than she felt Jock had, but like everyone else dutifully running the stalls, she had smiled and said the right things... all in a good cause. She took Jock to join Eeyore out of the sun in the last remaining stable at Manor Farm, where he could lie down on the bed of straw if he wished. She fed him a reviving meal of horse nuts and made sure he was watered before she drove back to the fête.

While Eliza was stabling Jock, Annie was giggling as she had a go at the coconut shy, with every throw landing short and wide. She took hold of the next ball, but it never left her hand because a high-pitched scream echoed across the garden.

"Someone help me!" A look of terror on her face, long blonde hair flying, Stella tore across the lawn dodging stalls shrieking, "Someone help! Someone's killed my Baby! Someone's killed her."

In the folds of her chiffon cover-up she was clutching something wet to her chest.

Francesca reached her first and led her to a chair quickly brought forward by others. She gently prised Stella's arms away from her bosom to see what the terrified woman was holding. The little Chihuahua's head lolled, the tongue hung out, the eyes stared. Baby was very much dead.

"*Drunkna!* You see?" Stella burst into tears and sat howling in despair. It was obvious from the little animal's soaking corpse that it had drowned. By now a few people had gathered round to comfort the hysterical young woman while a larger group of onlookers stood fixated, watching the horror unfold.

Through uncontrollable sobs Stella managed to explain.

"I... I left her in the kitchen. I went to collect her for the dog fancy dress competition, but she was gone. Disappeared." She said she had run around the house and garden searching everywhere for her little dog. "And then, in the Contemplative Garden... At the bottom of the pond–" She broke off sobbing again.

Unable to think of anything to say and shocked by what Stella was saying, Francesca put her arms round her and clasped the distressed woman, whose fluency with the English language had slipped a bit at this time of crisis. "Somebody go and find Bob, *please!*" she announced.

A couple of men jumped into action and ran to Bob's clay pigeon shoot. Francesca did her best to calm the distraught woman. But Stella appeared not to hear.

"Oh, I cannot believe what I saw. My poor darling. She was just lying on bottom of pool. I will never forget."

"But if she was in the kitchen, how can that be?"

"I don't know. I don't know. Who would do this to my darling, to my Baby?"

"Who else was in the house, Stella?"

"No-one – everyone was at the fête. I don't think any other people were there. Unless they came in through the French windows, I guess."

"But were they open?"

"One was."

The huge state-of-the-art kitchen at Heronsford Manor had four sets of arched French windows opening onto the garden, and off it, a scullery, a gunroom and a downstairs lavatory off a passage that led to the back door.

It suddenly occurred to Francesca to ask, "Has Baby ever been swimming before?"

"She never went near water. She was terrified. Very frightened."

She broke off to stare at Baby who was now lying in her lap. The woman's head drooped in misery. Tears fell down her reddened cheeks. Francesca turned to glance at the gathered crowd of people clearly moved by the calamity. Like the red sea, it parted as Bob and Jay came running up the lawn.

"My angel! My darling! Whatever has happened?"

Bob was on his knees on the grass beside Stella's chair. "How can this be?"

Jay gasped in horror at the sight of the chihuahua while Bob gently removed Baby from Stella's lap. He was about to take the body away when a further wail came from Stella. "Don't you dare take my Baby away! You leave my Baby with me!"

Francesca squatted down to look Stella in the face. She gently took hold of her arm.

"Stella, Bob's just going to wrap up Baby and put her somewhere safe. That's all. He's just going to take her away from all this... to some privacy in the house. Shall we go with him?"

Katie and her children arrived. Melissa Nicholson said, "Can I do anything to help?"

This appeared to bring Stella back from her despair and she replied, "You are kind, Melissa. Thank you for your kindness. You can come to the house with me? I cannot go into that house alone."

"You could have a proper funeral for Baby. And bury her in a special place in your garden."

"I need to find the bastard... beast who do this." She started to sob again.

"How about calling the police? They could test for DNA and fingerprints," Johnny was displaying the first hint of eagerness he had shown all holiday.

Katie interjected, "Yes, that's a good idea."

Stella shrugged. Through red-rimmed eyes smudged with mascara, she looked sadly at Katie. "Bob, I think would not want the police here, he didn't..." she paused, "he only likes big dogs like Fritz."

"Well, how about we suggest it to him?" said Katie.

"Yes, let's do that," Francesca echoed.

This was the first time Francesca and Katie had realised that all might not be well between Stella and Bob and they both wondered about this.

Katie told the children to wait behind while she and Francesca linked arms with Stella and led the trembling woman to follow Bob into her house. They went into the kitchen where Bob had found a cardboard box, wrapped the dog in a towel and put it in the box. Stella peered over the box and like a toreador, removed the towel with a flourish and pointed, "You see? You see?" she shrieked, "Something has broken her neck! Look! How could someone do this to an animal and to my poor little Baby?"

Head flopping, eyes staring, mouth open, tongue lolling out, now the others saw what Stella was saying. The chihuahua had clearly had its neck broken and had presumably been thrown into the pond.

Bob said quietly, "It looks like another dog got hold of her, angel. There are quite a few here."

"Or Fritz?"

"Fritz would never touch Baby, you know that."

"Well," said Annie later to Eliza. "I will say this: whatever or whoever killed the dog, chose a good day to do it. There were over a hundred people and dog suspects at the fête."

"And that's another dead body in water," said Eliza. "Things are going from bad to worse in this village."

"Hmm. Could there be a link to Louise's death?" wondered Annie.

12

LATE JULY

Patrick and his daughter were sorting out the house, readying for their move to Cambridge in August. The sale on Sparepenny Place would not be completed until late November, so they were leaving a few of their least essential things to be collected later.

"Don't forget to bring everything with you that you will need in the next three months."

"Of course, I won't," Sinead snapped at him. The more she had to rely on him since her mother's death, the angrier she felt that he was the one of her parents left alive. Since her mother's horrible death, she refused to go near the swimming pool, feeling faintly nauseous every time she had to glimpse it in the garden. Unanswered questions buzzed inside her head that she kept to herself. Her feelings had become distorted. She knew it wasn't logical, but her twisted thoughts told her that her father was to blame. So, she sometimes felt, were all her mother's village friends.

While she was clearing her bedroom, she hid some things in an ancient tiny cupboard near the chimney in her room. Patrick put his head round the door. She slammed the cupboard door shut and he took it that it was something private she didn't want him to see.

"Oops, sorry, women's stuff," he smiled. "Wasn't snooping, just checking you're getting along okay?"

"I'm eleven, not six," Sinead growled. "I think I can manage to clear my room, thank you."

As he so often had to these days, Patrick slunk away from his daughter feeling a mix of hurt and pity. He prayed that time would do its stuff and that moving would be the first step to helping his poor child get through what had happened to her.

Louise's money was still working its way through the legal processes and the delay in completing the sale left them short. But Bob McKenzie had been only too happy to bridge the gap with a loan to Patrick.

For McKenzies, the Ryans' move was a win-win situation. They had two house sales going through in what was otherwise a bleak time for the housing market. Bob may have been generous and kind-hearted, but was a businessman through and through.

Since some things were too large for their new house, Patrick planned to sort out what to get rid of and what to keep. Apart from anything, he needed to clear Louise's clothes while Sinead was not around. But for now, they hung in their dusty wardrobe untouched.

Meanwhile, the rest of those in Heronsford who could afford to, took holidays. Bob and Stella visited friends on a Greek island while Katie and Hamish took their children for a week's holiday to Cornwall and then to stay with Hamish's parents in Dorset. Eliza managed to persuade Jay to visit his sister in Cheshire for a few days and Francesca took off to Italy to see family for a fortnight.

For adults, the British weather was hot, sticky and uncomfortable, particularly for those who did not enjoy heat. But for the school-children who spent a large amount of time splashing about in hastily purchased, blown-up paddling pools, parents were grateful that they could let them spend days out of doors and out of their way.

Events and the school holidays meant Eliza had forgotten her insistence on taking Annie to the doctor. The woman's back got worse and she finally made an appointment and took herself to the village surgery. Just as Eliza had suspected, Dr Gordon had diagnosed osteoarthritis and prescribed painkillers.

Various people with children invited Sinead over for days or to stay for a few nights. Patrick had to go back to manning the shop in Cambridge and when no other option was available, he took Sinead with him.

As it does in England, once the heat had mounted, the air became humid and heavy. This accumulated over four days and eventually gave way to a big thunderstorm that raged over Heronsford, strafing its houses and land with hailstones. A deluge followed. It came down as though some vast invisible dam above had burst its walls. When the rain abated, the air cleared and the inhabitants felt the first relief since the shroud of heat had draped itself over the country during the latter half of June.

Popping in to see her mother on Friday morning, as Eliza walked past Annie's Ford Fiesta, she noticed vicious key marks criss-crossed and etched deeply along one side. She found the same thing on the other side as well as another couple on the rear door. These violent scratches implied rage... but against Annie? There wasn't a person around who had anything but love or at least admiration for Annie, so Eliza guessed it must have happened in Cambridge. That anyone would pick out such an insignificant, everyday car to violate was strange. Unless Annie parked somewhere she should not have done? Her daughter thought this quite likely since the old girl was getting a bit absent-minded lately.

"Mum, did you know that your car has been keyed right along both sides?"

"Keyed? What is keyed? What do you mean?"

"Scratched with a key. Deliberately. It has three deep lines along both sides of it. I'm so sorry, Mum. Any idea when it could have happened?"

"Oh dear! I must go and have a look." Annie walked to her front door and out to the car parked nearby. She walked round the car and stood gazing at the damage in surprise.

"Kids, Mum, punk kids," said Eliza, following her back into the house. "Must have happened recently as it definitely wasn't like that on Thursday. Been into Cambridge?"

Such matters did not much bother Annie. Taking it in her stride, she said she had only been to Heronsford to have lunch with her friend Pam on Thursday and to the village shop and then church on Sunday morning but nowhere else.

That was strange but Eliza didn't want to harp on it and worry the old girl. "'Fraid it will mean a trip to Thompsons. What a bore for you, Mum."

"Oh well. Not sure I'll bother, darling." For Annie, a car was a machine for getting from A to B, not something to be proud of or that warranted much care, as long as it worked. What interested her more was who the culprit might be. She thought about whom she had seen in the village when she'd had lunch followed by the habitual games of chess with Pam on Thursday. She had parked in Pam's driveway while she had lunch and she had stayed for an hour or so afterwards playing her favourite game with her friend. She thought it unlikely anyone had carried out this pitifully vicious act then.

She thought back to when she had visited the village shop on Sunday morning to get her paper, as did many in Heronsford. Katie Nicholson had been in the shop and when Annie had left, she had seen the Nicholson children milling about outside. Could it have been one of them? Unlikely in broad daylight, when anyone could have caught them at it.

"And then I went to matins," she told Eliza. "There were just a few older people there." The congregation was decreasing all the time.

While Annie would say that her churchgoing was purely out of a sense of duty to the village, perhaps it was also an old habit. Childhood bedtime prayers, Bible readings, Sunday school and books about Jesus had left an invisible imprint on her young brain.

Later, the left hemisphere of that brain rejected religion, but its limbic system retained memories that still propelled her towards maintaining some tiny connection with her childhood. She attended matins about once a month but never took communion.

Eliza's ancestors and Annie's husband were buried in the graveyard of that church. She felt strongly that while people such as herself happily buried their old, christened their young, married one another and went along to the Christmas carol service as much for the camaraderie as the mince pies afterwards, that the institution deserved supporting. And if the heavenly grace it purported to impart was less rewarding to her than her contribution to the collection box was to it, the fact did not bother her at all.

Annie decided that it might have been during the Sunday service that some likely village lads had walked past her car and left their macho little marks of aggression.

That week Pam Sowerby brought her West Highland Terrier to lunch with Annie B. After lunch, they took their little dogs for a walk before the obligatory games of chess.

They walked across the field in front of Rooks Wood. Instead of taking Annie's usual route through the wood, since it was post-harvest, they followed the path round to its right. They walked along the east side of the wood where they followed the edge of the stubble field round to make their way back along the other side. Round bales of barley straw like giant corks dotted the flat surface. Occasional scraggy poppies had made a brave appearance. Fascinated by the nests of mice exposed by the combine, the dogs snuffled through the six-inch high cut stalks.

The usual village matters happily relegated to bottom of the Heronsford gossip agenda, the women discussed the latest horrible event to have happened in the village.

Earlier that week, Rose had come to clean Annie's house and had been very shaken up. "I'm all right, Mrs Berkeley," she'd told Annie, "but someone has destroyed my front garden."

"Destroyed? Good Heavens, Rose. Whatever do you mean?"

Annie knew Rose tended her little front garden with devoted care and she had been so proud of the petunias, lobelias, marigolds, marguerites and other bedding plants she put in every summer.

"They beheaded every single flower and left the heads in a pile by the front door," said the woman, obviously shocked to the core.

She was shocked indeed, Annie saw, and frightened too. As she cleaned she chattered on about her feelings. As far as she knew, she had never had an enemy in the village. Why and how such a thing had happened had greatly distressed Rose. Annie had done her best to comfort her.

"It has to be the same child or children who damaged your car, Annie," said Pam.

"Well, yes, indeed it could be." Years as a barrister defending both the innocent and the guilty had taught Annie that nothing is ever as obvious as it seems. "But then again," she added, "it could be an adult with a grudge or a mental problem. In fact, there are a number of possibilities."

"But surely a grown up wouldn't do anything so ridiculous as scratching the paint on your car and cutting the heads off plants?"

"I don't believe one can ever be sure that an adult would not do something equally as silly or sillier than a child."

As they made their way back to Manor Farm Barn, the two women continued to discuss these nasty occurrences and the sad death of Louise.

"I still think there was foul play there," said Annie, "and I have my suspicions about who the perpetrator might be."

"Ooh, do tell, Annie."

"I have no proof, just suspicion at the moment, and it wouldn't be fair for me to say anything. But one thing I will say. Where a pretty young woman is involved, sex is often a motive."

29 July

That last Sunday in July was family only at Manor Farm for lunch. This included Annie. They ate cold chicken mayonnaise and salad followed by strawberries, raspberries, blueberries and cream in the kitchen as it was now too hot to eat outside. Everyone was beginning to suffer from the oppressive heat, Annie especially, but she made no mention of it. Most of the family had taken to sleeping downstairs on sofas due to the slightly cooler atmosphere.

Once the adults had finished discussing the week's politics, always a subject to interest Annie, the conversation came around to the horrible end of Stella's little dog. They were not alone in their interest in this most bizarre event as most of Heronsford was talking about it. Annie said, "I saw Bob with the little dog at the fête."

"You what?"

"I saw him carrying the dog under his arm. At the fête. He was walking across the garden."

"You don't think? Surely not?"

"Darling, I only know what I saw." She paused. "What makes it worse is that poor girl's desire for a child."

Not wanting to dwell on such matters in front of Holly, Eliza changed the subject. "Anyway, it looks like good news is on the horizon for us. John Spencer have said that they are considering making an order for autumn, although not yet how many. So, fingers crossed, we could be back in business again."

Annie almost sang the words, "That is just wonderful. Oh, I'm so pleased." She went quite pink. "In fact, this has made my day. Worthy of a toast I think." Steadying herself on the table edge, she got slowly to her feet, the pain showing on her face. She raised her wine glass and in mock formality, looked at the family and said, "Will you all please charge your glasses..."

Giggling, Holly poured a bit more Coca Cola into her glass, allowed on Sundays during the holidays. Juliet, who was permitted wine on Sundays, offered some to Eliza and Jay and then topped up her glass too. Once that was done, Annie continued, "I want you to know that I love you all very much indeed and that I shall never stop doing so. Times have not been easy, but you have steered the ship along the right course and made it through. So ladies and gentleman, I ask you to raise your glasses to Eliza Berkeley Designs," she paused and added quietly, "and all who sail in her."

"To Eliza Berkeley Designs and all who sail in her!"

Eliza got up to go around the table and hug her mother. "You're the figurehead on this ship, Mum, and don't you forget it. We would never have left port without you."

Jay jumped up from his chair. He pointed a trembling finger at his mother-in-law and shouted, "The order is not confirmed. They are only considering it. What do you think you are saying, figurehead Annie?"

Taken aback, Annie sat down quickly. "I'm so sorry, Jay. I just assumed..."

"Well, don't! Don't assume, thank you very much. Keep your toasts to yourself," the man was shrieking.

"Jay!" Red in the face, Eliza comforted her mother who looked aghast.

"I think I'd better leave. Thank you for a lovely lunch. Again, I'm so sorry, Jay. I really didn't mean to upset you." Annie rose quietly to her feet and left the stunned family to cope with the aftermath of Jay's eruption.

When she got back to the barn the realisation dawned on her that her son-in-law harboured a grudge towards her. Unfair though it certainly was to make her the scapegoat for his own failings, she knew that since he had come under so much stress, it was obvious from his outburst that he resented her. For her presence or for the gift of the farm, she was not sure. But felt it, she did.

13

4 AUGUST

"And Francesca and Stella will be there," Katie added. Eliza was relieved when Katie phoned that evening to invite her and the children to a barbecue on Saturday. She'd had Sinead staying for the past three nights and the adult Armstrongs found communicating with her a big struggle.

They were proud of Holly who dealt with the devastated child far more naturally than they did, and in consequence, Sinead was more at ease with her. Eliza had tried comforting her but the only woman aside from her grandmother the girl would allow to get close was Francesca. The child had turned inward and changed from being an outgoing kid to sulky and resentful. Her sorrow infiltrated those who tried to help.

The tragedy of Louise, business problems, Jay's anxiety, the hot, humid days and the summer holiday were beginning to take a toll on Eliza's patience, and she looked forward to some adult company. Bob, Jay and Hamish had planned a day's fly fishing for trout at Rutland Water on Saturday, meaning it would be entirely feminine company for a change. She looked forward to it.

Holly, Sinead, the two Nicholson children and the four women all crowded round the Nicholsons' slatted garden table that was intended to seat six at the most.

An ancient faded green parasol was slotted through a hole in its middle and open above it. It leant at a drunken angle to the table. No-one had any elbowroom, but they didn't mind and even Stella, used to the total opposite in her enormous house, seemed to enjoy the feel of friends crammed together. The others didn't know it but she was reminded of her large, happy Swedish family who'd had little money but big appetites.

Katie had made a variety of salads and served them with marinated chicken and sausages cooked on the barbecue. They ate off white Eliza Berkeley plates with comical red and yellow chickens cavorting round the rim. Happy music came through the open kitchen doors from a speaker. Katie loved dancing and her thing was eighties disco music. They all sang along.

Francesca was excited to have landed a role in a West End London play that was to start rehearsals the following month. Everyone congratulated her and toasted her success.

Sinead seemed more relaxed than she had been since her mother's death.

Johnny was fourteen, spotty, difficult and completely self-absorbed in his adolescence. Going the same way, Melissa, was twelve. They had both become more egocentric since going to Broxton College and Katie felt a tinge of sadness for the lost days of unsophistication. Now, they were iPad addicts. They knew they knew best and in spite of all the early lessons in manners, sometimes answered back. The worst thing was that Johnny in particular had become bored with country living. But today, even Johnny forgot to be bolshie and joined in some of the conversations. But he reverted when he laughed and pointed out something moving in front of Francesca's plate. Across the table, Stella tipped her chair back and almost screamed, "Spider...!"

Then they all saw it. It was huge. It was hairy and black, more tarantula than spider. When Francesca realised, she cried out in shock as she jumped up from the table. As she did the creature moved slowly to the edge of the table and dropped onto the ground. Everyone jumped to their feet to look for it. In the commotion this had caused, a wine glass had been knocked over and broken so there was glass everywhere.

Katie had been scared too but now she shrieked, "It's okay! It's okay, Francesca, it's a toy. It's not a real tarantula. Remote control." She was so furious she could barely get her words out. She stood up and shouted at Johnny. "You silly little idiot! That was really frightening. I have had enough of your appalling behaviour. Enough! You understand? Say you're sorry at once. Say you're really sorry and apologise at once. And don't ever do anything like that again."

Johnny had never heard his mother so cross. He realised that his so-called joke had gone way beyond such a thing and had caused genuine upset round the table. He looked ashamed. Francesca's dramatic cry and his mother's rage so alarmed him that he apologised profusely to Francesca and asked if there was anything he could do to help.

Her adrenalin firing, her staginess at the fore, Francesca replied, "I tell you what, darling boy, in future just make it your business to develop a bit more feeling toward others. It will stand you in very good stead."

"I'm really sorry, Francesca, I only meant it as a joke." The child was crimson and hung his head.

Katie went into the kitchen to find a dustpan and brush while Eliza and Stella stayed with the unnerved Francesca: spiders were one of her chief fears. But another glass of wine soon helped restore her equilibrium and she was by now well on the way to being sloshed.

Defusing the situation, Katie called Johnny to help her bring out the dessert and everyone forgot the incident. Music blasting from behind her, Katie came out of the kitchen carrying a tray and dancing and singing raucously along to the track.

All the women joined in and got up to clap and dance while Katie put the desserts on the rickety table.

But they soon sat down again to wolf Katie's delicious Eton mess, ginger snaps and wonderful home-made lemon ice cream.

After lunch, the children wandered off into the house and left the women to their coffee and more rosé that Francesca and Katie quaffed as though it was juice.

Francesca remarked on the difference in Sinead and the others were in agreement.

"I think she may be beginning to get used to it," said Eliza, "although it's easier for her in the holidays with everyone helping out. It'll be very tough on the poor child when she starts at St Paul's next term."

"It's good she has Holly with her," said Stella who had been more comfortable during lunch than any of them had seen her before. She joined in more than usual and appeared to be enjoying herself. The other females' antennae tingled with the knowledge that her husband wasn't around.

"Poor Patrick is struggling," said Eliza.

"At least he'll never find out about her affair now–" Stopping short, Francesca remembered Louise had confided in her, not about who he was, but about the fact that she was seeing someone. She had forgotten Sinead was around and her cheeks flushed.

The three other women sat forward. Katie whispered, "An affair?"

"Heavens!" Eliza looked around to make sure Sinead was out of earshot. "Who with?"

"The naughty girl!" Stella said softly.

"Oh, my big mouth. I'm such a blabber-fool."

"Don't worry," said Eliza. "It's usually me. Anyway, sweetheart, it can't do any harm to anyone now. Unless Sinead or Patrick were to find out."

"I shouldn't have mentioned it. Louise told me in confidence. It hadn't been going on long and I really don't know whom it was with. She wouldn't say."

Stella suddenly chipped in, "Then why the hell did she kill herself?"

The women stopped speaking and looked at one another.

Then Katie said, "But the police investigated and found nothing to suggest any foul play."

"True," said Eliza. "Surely they'd have found something – DNA or something. Your imagination running away with you there, Stella?" Realising too late that she had sounded patronising, she smiled at the younger woman to reassure her she had not intended to.

The subject hung heavy over the garden table and, overwhelmed by the heat, food, wine, lack of energy but most of all the reminder of Louise's death, the women found it difficult to find the wherewithal to get to their feet and clear away the table. But they managed and the doing of it lifted the atmosphere again.

"By the way, you're all invited – plus hubbies – to Smith's on Friday evening. It's my birthday!" said Francesca.

"I'm nineteen and I know you are younger than me, so I guess you are eighteen, yes?" Stella surprised everyone: she was seldom noted for her humour.

"Nail on the spot, my darling!"

"Why not let us take you out instead?" said Eliza.

"No, no, no – you're all coming to me and that's that," she lurched as she stood up. "Must go to the loo. Don't suppose the lawn needs watering?" Clutching her crotch like a small child, she had them all giggling as she teetered towards the house.

"Sorry, Francesca. Hamish is back tomorrow. He'll do it."

"I bet he will! I'd love to see his hose – let me know when he gets it out and I'll be here in a jiffy."

Eliza said nothing.

Happier than any of them had ever seen her before, Stella hooted with laughter. She appeared genuinely to have enjoyed herself and kissed them all goodbye with more warmth than they had experienced from her before. She helped them clear the table and carry the plates and glasses through to the kitchen before she departed, waving to them all.

Katie felt pleased with herself for inviting her as she saw how much it had meant to her. She said as much to Eliza and Francesca, who agreed they had never seen the woman so relaxed before.

"Got away from Bob. That's why." Francesca could be relied on to voice the unspoken thoughts of others.

Eliza grimaced and nodded, "She is, after all, about half his age... And a Swede living in a huge country house, miles from anywhere – wouldn't be exactly surprising, would it?" she said.

"Suppose it wouldn't, and the poor lamb has just lost her 'baby' in the most horrible of circumstances. Now she has even more reason to be unhappy."

"That was such an awful, dreadful thing. Has she got any nearer finding out who did it?"

"No, I don't think she has."

"We must try to involve her with us more. She's really rather sweet."

Eliza insisted on driving Francesca home. "You're far too smashed to negotiate the lanes," she said. "I'll come and get you tomorrow so you can pick up your car."

"Good," said Francesca. She hiccupped. "I'll give you lunch and you can help me rehearse my lines for the new play." The children snickered in the back of the car.

Eliza and the children watched Francesca in her red stilettos waver down the tiny path to her cottage, brandishing her keys in the air before failing a few times to aim the door key into its keyhole. They remained watching and giggling until she finally managed, and half fell through the door into her cottage.

"She's had too much to drink, hasn't she?" said Holly. Sinead glowered.

"I think she's just had a bit too much sun," said Eliza.

"Come on, Mum. She's drunk, isn't she?" Both girls snorted.

"Well, she's tired and..." Eliza delayed her response with a pause. "Perhaps she may have had a glass too many."

They drove back to Manor Farm and within half an hour Patrick arrived to collect Sinead and take her back to Cambridge.

Intended for a late sandwich never eaten, the bacon curled, crisped, blackened and broke into slivers of charcoal while the fat boiled, spat and splattered over the pan's edge.

Annie had been invited by Pam to supper. They picked at their ham, potato salad and green salad, agreeing their appetites had diminished in the hot weather. Pam noted her friend's face had caught the sun. A bossy woman, she told Annie to make sure to keep it out of the sun.

Annie already did this and wore hats whenever she went outside in the sunshine, but she didn't bother to say. She had known Pam a long time. A person who knew best, she could not be told and that was that. She had qualities that, as far as Annie was concerned, made up for times when she was overbearing, and even these were generally well intended. Speaking her mind as usual, Pam just about ordered Annie to see Edward Gordon. Assuring her she was taking anti-inflammatory pills as well as the occasional painkiller, Annie added, "Although I don't like taking pills if I don't absolutely have to."

"That's plain daft, Annie. If you're hurting, take the pills. That's what they're for."

They played chess later than they usually allowed themselves and it was after 11pm by the time Annie drove herself home through the village. When she looked in the mirror later, she saw what Pam meant.

Her face did seem to be more golden than its usual English-rose look and she supposed she must have caught more sun than she had intended. She made a note to herself to be more careful.

Hamish returned very late, stocked with trout and happy from a good day out followed by a fine meal that generous Bob had insisted on paying for.

Katie was in a deep, snoring sleep long before Hamish got home. She didn't stir when he tiptoed into the bedroom. But in spite of the big man's attempt to be as quiet as possible, she woke up when the bed sagged under his weight.

He had turned onto his side and gone straight to sleep. Katie lay in the dark for a while, the events of the day passing through her mind once more. It had been a fun lunch and she again congratulated herself for inviting Stella. But, in spite of her headache, sleep now refused her permission to re-enter.

She knew Hamish loved her, but they had been married for fourteen years. While he made no obvious show of liking or admiring other women, the finest nuances are seldom lost on wives when it comes to their husbands' reactions to attractive women and she was well aware that sometimes Hamish failed to hide it from her.

He'd had after all, she told herself, very limited time to sow his wild oats before they had married as she had become pregnant. She felt his broad body lying with his back to her and manoeuvred her own next to his. He always gave off body heat and even with only a sheet to cover them, the bed was becoming surprisingly warm.

Wrapping a soft arm round his waist, she held her man for a while then lowered her hand to his sleeping penis. She held and massaged it gently, hoping he would respond. "You awake, Hami?" She hoped he would answer. He stirred to move her hand away and mumbled something about being too tired.

She had known that from the way he stood that tiny bit taller and became that fraction more gallant and shown a tinge of extra interest in what she said that he had fancied Louise. But had he taken it further than that? Katie couldn't get the idea out of her aching mind.

A roll of J-cloths lying close to the gas ring caught. Within seconds, one flame became more, the greediest reaching out to lick its tongue around the nearby roll of kitchen paper on its stand. Some wooden spoons in a small crock on the worktop were the next to go.

At about the same time that Hamish was falling asleep beside Katie, Bob was hammering his sex into his wife from behind.

Out of the ordinary for the sound sleeper she was, at around 11.20pm, one of Francesca's neighbours woke up. She sat up in bed and listened. She got out of bed and tiptoed to the bedroom window. She opened the curtain a chink, unlatched the window and peered out at the darkness. To the left she saw an orange glow and a large rat scuttle away down the lane.

Following a good Saturday night out with some pals at the Chinese restaurant in the small town of Broxton, Nick and Sally Baker had been asleep for over an hour when a sound like a swarm of angry bees woke them at around quarter past midnight.

Nick silenced the pager and jumped out of bed. He threw on

some clothes, snatched up the pager again and left the room before Sally had time to ask. Pocketing the pager, he raced the quarter mile on foot to the station. He knew from experience that it was quicker than taking the car and finding a parking space for it.

He grabbed his helmet and boots from the locker, acknowledged the driver and was the first to climb up into the rear seats. Three other men and one woman, still securing their outfits, came running to join him. In moments the vast vehicle drove slowly out of its garage, majestic as its siren climbed loud octaves before screaming on. Blue lights on its top, side and headlights flashing, it turned right and began to pick up speed.

It was a clear road and they reached the village in less than ten minutes, but by the time they got to the address, they could see there was little hope. Roaring, the roof had already caught. This was going to be no easy task to control. Straightaway, they called the Cambridge Fire Station for backup. Their main anxiety was the considerable danger of other houses catching.

In those vital minutes before the brigade had reached the fire, the woman who had first seen the fire from her bedroom along with others who had seen the blaze along the lane, had run out in their dressing gowns to see if they could help.

Two men and a woman had managed to get as near to the front door as they could. But hot clouds of smoke were escaping from the cracks around it. Before they had attempted to get in, flames had streamed out of an open window upstairs, flared upwards and caught the roof. The place had gone up so fast it was terrifying to watch. Onlookers had gasped with horror and backed away as it had burned with fury, the intensity of the heat and smoke filling the air and choking their lungs.

Their powerlessness had angered and upset them and in the short time it took the fire brigade to arrive, the hope of saving occupants was lost.

All the firefighters could do was attempt to douse the flames and be glad the neighbouring cottages and houses had not been affected apart from some singeing and dirtying from the dark smoke.

In the end it took five teams several hours to control the blaze.

The exhausted Nick, who doubled as the local electrician, muttered to himself in anger, "If only people would spray these old roofs with fire retardant."

It took them until 6am to finally put the fire out. All that remained of Smith's Cottage was a shell, the old brick chimneystack standing alone among its broken walls.

It was then that the firemen brought out a body bag.

14

5–6 AUGUST

Eliza felt more refreshed in the morning than she had for some time. Dialling a call on her landline, she was also making the second pot of coffee of the morning. After a few rings a woman answered. In unemotional language, she said, "Sorry. The service requested is not available. Thank you for calling. Please hang up."

After trying again but receiving the same recording, Eliza tried another number. The response told her that number was not available either. Puzzled, Eliza tried it once more.

Annie implemented the obligatory knock agreed to when she and her daughter had become such close neighbours. Without waiting for a "come in", she walked through the back door into the kitchen. She sat down on a kitchen chair and waited for her daughter's attention. Although her daughter didn't notice, by looking closely at her expression, you might have seen that Annie seemed anxious.

"Was that Francesca you were trying?"

"It was, as it happens." The sarcasm and irritation were not lost on her mother.

"Well, I'm so sorry to disturb you, sweetheart, but Rose has told me some very bad news that I thought you should know as soon as possible."

"What's happened?"

"Sit down, darling. Sit down."

Eliza sat on a chair next to her mother. A sense of panic beginning to take hold, she studied her mother's face, but years of court performances ensured it revealed nothing.

In a small saucepan, the milk heated on the warm plate of the Aga. It grew hot and formed a skin.

"Tell me, Mum."

Annie put her hand on her daughter's arm and cleared her throat. "It seems that Smith's Cottage caught fire last night."

Eliza stared at her. Annie allowed the fact to sink in.

"Was Francesca there?"

"She was."

"Oh God. Oh God. Tell me she's okay?"

Annie slowly shook her head. Eliza looked at her in disbelief. Going pale, she said, "She's in hospital?"

The thin white skin developed and stretched until it became an air-filled bubble that grew and shuddered when the fluid below rose up like a tiny tsunami to burst its way over the top of saucepan. But neither woman noticed.

Annie grabbed her daughter's hand and held it tight. She fixed her eyes on her face and said with unhurried but gentle purpose, "She didn't make it, Eliza. She died in the fire." She quickly stood up, stepped behind her daughter's chair, encircled her arms around her child's body and held her firm while Eliza absorbed then broke.

Using special infrared equipment designed to trace the origins or "hot-spot" of the blaze, after searching through the remains of Smith's Cottage, the fire service announced that the fire came from a gas cooker that had been left on. They could even tell that a pan of food had been the culprit. But to be sure the fire was not started deliberately, they took bits of debris from the scene for analysis.

Everyone in the village was in shock. A second unnatural death within two months had shaken it to its foundations. People who lived close by and saw the fire were traumatised. And for days to come, the villagers spoke of nothing else.

On the way back from seeing Pam the previous evening, Annie had seen something that had disturbed her. It bothered her so much that she paid a visit to the Parkside Police to report what she had seen.

While Louise's death was dreadful, it had been of her own choosing and she had not been particularly involved with the village, preferring to keep herself apart. On the other hand, Francesca's death was a terrible accident. To choke to death in such appalling circumstances must have been terrifying for the poor young woman who had been popular with everyone who knew her. She had always been cheerful and smiling and had made people laugh. "Sunny" was how some described her, and it had suited her well. People had revelled in the fact that they had a television star living in their midst and they would really miss her. For a short time, the press descended on the village asking questions and taking photographs.

THE CAMBRIDGE NEWS

Castleton Actress Dies in Tragic Heronsford Fire

Francesca Bianchi, 39, the actress who appeared in *Castleton* as Becky Harper in the first decade of the twenty-first century, as well as taking roles in many television series such as *Tenby City* and *The Force,* died last night in a blazing fire that all but destroyed her entire cottage in the village of Heronsford near Cambridge.

Onlookers at the scene were shocked at how quickly the place went up, the thatch catching like tinder. Miss Bianchi was found dead by firefighters inside the burning property after they received a call at 23.40.

The fire started on the ground floor of the property and ripped through the first floor. At the peak of the blaze there were twelve firefighters present with four engines on the scene. The fire was finally extinguished by the early morning, but crews remained at the property, investigating. The cause of the fire is currently unknown. Cambridgeshire Constabulary are assisting the fire and rescue service with the probe.

A fire service statement said: "This particular fire presented crews with a number of difficult challenges." Assistant Chief Fire Officer Mike Andrews praised members of the

DATE // DAY // ISSUE NUMBER

public who called them and tried to help stem the fire. He also highlighted the courageous operational response from firefighters at Broxton Fire Station and the Cambridge Fire and Rescue service. "An investigation continues into the cause of the fire in conjunction with the police while crews remain on site damping down any hotspots and making sure the area is safe." Mike Andrews added. "That no other buildings were affected apart from singeing is a miracle."

The vicar of Heronsford said, "I think I can say I speak for us all when I tell you that Miss Bianchi, or Francesca as she encouraged people to call her, was a highly popular, dynamic and colourful member of the village. This is a great tragedy for our community, and for the world of theatre. Our thoughts and prayers are with the Bianchi family at this terrible time."

Mrs Eliza Armstrong, a close friend of Francesca's told us, "Cesca was the life and soul of our many happy times together. Full of laughter and fun, there was never a dull moment in her company. We shall miss her dreadfully. All of us who loved her are completely heartbroken by her loss. Coming as it does so fast on the heels of the tragic drowning in June of another friend, Mrs Louise Ryan, those of us left in the group of local friends are simply reeling with grief." See page 3, Francesca Bianchi dies.

THE GUARDIAN

Castleton Actress Dies in House Fire

Francesca Bianchi, the actress, has died in a house fire at her home at the age of 39. The old thatched cottage where she lived in the village of Heronsford, eight miles south of Cambridge, caught fire sometime before midnight on 4 August. By the time firefighters reached the scene, the cottage was ablaze, too late to save Miss Bianchi, who, it is thought, was asleep in bed when the fire started.

An Italian by birth, she was the only child of the owners of a well-known London restaurant, Fredo's in South Kensington. Miss Bianchi became quite the star attraction of the place where she learnt early the power of being centre stage. She was allowed and encouraged by her parents to roam the floor while people were eating. The pretty little girl would go from table to table enchanting diners with her delightful appeal, even when she was once in trouble for going under a table and filling a male customer's dangling shoe with spaghetti Bolognese.

Aged eighteen, she went on to attend the Central School of Speech and Drama, and it was not long after she left that she was reeling in the acting parts. One of the first was the

THE GUARDIAN

part of Becky Harper, landlady of the Royal Oak in the TV soap opera *Castleton*, that she played for nearly five years and for which she won a Royal Television Society award in 2003. Following this, she appeared in television dramas including *Tenby City* and *The Force*.

Perhaps a little too shapely in these days when svelteness seems to win most leading roles in films and television, Miss Bianchi was nonetheless an excellent actress. Less well-known to the wider public are the many parts she played on stage in London that included Portia in the *Merchant of Venice* at the Old Vic in 2006, for which she won an Evening Standard Theatre Award for best actress. Amongst other leading London stage roles, she played Geraldine Barclay in *What the Butler Saw* at the Vaudeville in 2008 and in the first decade of the twenty-first century she played many others, including major parts in the films, *Dark Places*, *The Cook* and *Somewhere in the World*.

Her death was described as "a serious tragedy" by Robert Gilmore, a friend and the producer of her last major television series, a 2009 comedy called *Down Devon Way*, in which she starred with Eddie Gwyn as a couple who drop out of the rat race to live in the country. He said, "It is rare to come across such a huge talent for both drama and comedy. Like all great actresses, as soon as she got on a stage or in front of the camera, she was absolutely mesmerising."

Having done as careful an external examination as possible of Francesca's remains and finding no evidence of injury, the pathologist's report declared no reason to assume any alternative cause of death other than the fire itself. It also commented on the presence of soot in the trachea, indicating that the woman had been alive when the fire started. The post-mortem results showed that she died from smoke inhalation. Samples of debris taken from the scene had been submitted and analysed by chemists to look for the presence of gasoline or any other ignitable fluid that might have been used to start the fire, but none was found.

15

MID TO LATE AUGUST

The two deaths were the talk of the village. Some people jumped to the conclusion that they were somehow linked. But others asked why or how they could be? Speculation was rampant and ludicrous stories started to circulate. Louise and Francesca Bianchi had been having a lesbian affair, being the most popular.

Annie Berkeley had a strong feeling that the theory about the deaths being linked held water. She wondered about all the members of her daughter's group of friends and, since her years in court had convinced her that there was naught so strange as folk, her naturally analytic mind asked her to consider various possibilities as to whether both deaths had in fact been murder. She also believed the motives to have been related to sex. She racked her brains and drew her own conclusions.

Like many other women in Heronsford, but more so because of what had happened to her garden, Rose became quite paranoid. She decided there was a local serial killer and told Annie B. as much. Competent as Rose was, she was subject to reacting to situations without thinking things through.

Annie calmed her over her worst fears and assured her she didn't believe either she or Rose were on the agenda of any murderer, local or not. This only went some way to allaying Rose's gravest worries. After Louise Ryan had died, Rose had walked to and fro to Sparepenny Place to clean and help out with Sinead, but now she stopped walking on her own anywhere and would only go out in her car. Other women were doing the same thing. Everyone had become wary.

The Armstrongs and the Nicholsons were invited to the McKenzie's for a dinner one evening. The mood was sober and their conversation was dominated by Francesca's death.

Everyone had their opinion. Near to tears, Eliza who had seen Francesca enter her cottage in a drunken state, said she believed it was a simple accident.

"If only I'd insisted she came back to the farm for the night. She really wasn't in a fit state to leave on her own. I blame myself."

Sitting next to her, Bob put his arm round her shoulders and pulled her toward him. He kissed her cheek.

"Of course it wasn't your fault, sweet girl. Francesca was a grown up, responsible for herself."

Then Stella chipped in. "I should have suggested she came home when I left a little earlier than the others. She was quite pissed by then, but apparently, she drank even more after I'd left. I just didn't think to do so."

Sitting next to her, in a reassuring gesture, Hamish rubbed a hand gently on her back. "It wasn't your fault either, Stell. Don't even dream that it was."

Because they were all now beginning to be suspicious of one another, few could say what they really thought.

But in the black and white way that was Bob's, he was utterly convinced that Patrick had something to do with both deaths. While they all liked Patrick, they could see that Bob had a point.

Walking home with her husband that evening, Katie Nicholson

welled up with misery and anger. Now she felt sure that Hamish was having an affair with Stella. What made it even worse was how beautiful Stella was. She had to watch them pretending to avoid one another when they were so obviously involved.

She stopped suddenly in the middle of the lane and screamed at Hamish, "How could you, you cheating bastard?" She dropped her handbag on the road and set about pummelling his chest and throwing wild punches at him.

Astonished by the ferocity of this attack, Hamish backed away and caught hold of her forearms. He held her tightly and away from him. "What are you talking about, Katie? Whatever is the matter? What do you mean, cheating? Explain yourself!"

"Do you think I'm a complete fool? I know you're having an affair with Stella. It's so, so obvious!"

"An affair with Stella? You're joking, Katie. Tell me you're joking."

She tried to wriggle free from his grasp with no luck. "I can read between the lines, you know. I saw the way you kissed her goodbye and the way you were looking at each other and feigning indifference. I saw you patting her back. You clearly can't keep your hands off the woman. You must think I'm a complete bloody fool, Hamish."

"As it just so happens, in this instance, that's exactly what I do think. Wherever you got that idea from, God knows, Katie. You drink far too much, and your brain gets addled. I would no more go near Stella than jump off the top of Mount Everest. Besides, Bob would kill any man who did."

"So, you do fancy her! There you've admitted it. You can protest all you like but I know what I saw, and I know you're having an affair."

Hamish was shouting now. "I admitted nothing because there is nothing to admit! Stella is beautiful but that doesn't mean I fancy her. In fact, I don't at all. She's so not my type."

"Discussing your types now then? Don't think you have fooled me, Hamish. Because you haven't."

"Sweetheart, can we please calm down and talk about this

tomorrow when we're both sober? I swear to you on my grandfather's grave, I am not having an affair with Stella. Nor has it ever been something I have contemplated. You have to believe me, Katie. We have talked about your issues with jealousy before and this is another bout that has probably been brought on by the dreadful events in the village. It has made everyone feel unsettled and worried. Here, take my hand and let's go home."

Crying all the way, she allowed him to lead her back to Wood Farm. When they got home, Hamish was grateful to find the children had gone to bed. He half carried their drunken mother upstairs, undressed and helped her into bed. He then undressed himself and got in beside her. He held her until she fell asleep. The side of Katie that had showed itself this evening was horrible. He had seen it before, but never as bad as this. She had behaved like some crazed banshee. He lay awake, sleep refusing to come to him.

16

21 SEPTEMBER

The Met Office issued the weather alert at 6am on 21 September. A storm was expected to roll in from the Atlantic bringing gusts of up to 80mph. Forecasters warned of danger to life from flying debris, while power cuts, damage to buildings, road closures and transport cancellations were also predicted.

On the day of Francesca's funeral, Eliza, Jay, Katie and Hamish left their children under the far from watchful eye of a girl from the village. Bob had been unable to make it due to McKenzie's annual general meeting, but Stella, Patrick and Sinead joined them, and Annie too, in spite of her pain. They decided to beat the storm by travelling up to London by train. They took cabs from the station, which dropped them across the road from the church.

They battled against the gale to cross Fulham Road. A sudden gust from behind turned inside out the large umbrella with which Patrick was sheltering Stella. Under the watchful stony gazes of St Peter and St Paul flanking the sides of a wide arch, they joined the throngs of people walking gratefully out of the storm through a pair of big wrought-iron gates under a tall five-storey brick tower. Above them in the middle of a four-lancet window, Christ the Redeemer blessed them. They passed down a long colonnade of ten carved pillars into the nave of Our Lady of Dolours.

They found pews about halfway down the church and sat down. There were service sheets on the shelves of the back of the pews in front of them. The church was already filling up with people. A large choir sang Monteverdi's *Vespers*, filling the building with a solemn and reverent atmosphere that affected people to hush and walk slowly to their pews with their heads bent.

Clad in black, both wearing hats, she with a veil over her face, Fredo and Maria Bianchi sat in the front pew on the right-hand side of the church. Their heads bowed, their bodies bent, even from the rear they emanated intense grief. To their left in the centre of the transept, covered in a white pall, the casket was topped with wreaths and a spray of white lilies, a large white church candle burning in front of it. The irony of this did not miss Eliza but she kept it to herself.

Beside the coffin, a small table bore a vase of red, blue, yellow, mauve and white flowers next to a large silver framed photograph of Francesca's smiling face. A wooden crucifix draped with a silver rosary necklace stood beside the picture along with a group of white candles, a leather-bound Bible, a doll and a snow globe enclosing a winter scene.

From the high vaulted, blue painted ceiling, Christ looked down from a crucifix with an expression of despair.

The church was packed. Francesca had had a lot of friends in theatre and television and her large family had come over from Italy to support her parents. The service included hymns, readings from old friends and Holy Communion, during which those who wanted could go up to the altar while the rest stayed in their pews listening to Verdi's "Libera Me" from his *Requiem*, sung by a soloist and the choir.

It was a long but moving funeral and the Heronsford friends were downcast by the tragedy of the event. After the final commendation when the priest sprinkled holy water on the coffin, a recorded version of "On Eagle's Wings" filled the big church. All those who had been struggling to contain their sorrow simply let go for the emotion of it. Of the men, only Hamish managed to hold it together while Patrick sobbed, and Jay quietly let a few tears roll.

As they left the church, the many who had attended piled back out onto Fulham Road where the wind was stronger than ever. The Heronsford friends had all previously agreed to avoid the post-funeral luncheon that was to take place at Fredo's restaurant. It was going to be full of old London friends and Italians, so they didn't feel they would be missed. They did wait outside the church to shake the hands of Francesca's stricken parents, who were grateful to see them and told Sinead how much her daughter had loved her.

To honour their dear friend, they had agreed to have lunch in another restaurant in Kensington, where they planned to toast her and be happy for her sake. But as they made their way there, tension ran through the group. They all wished they had gone straight home and that they hadn't made this arrangement for lunch, but none knew how to voice it. Hamish seemed especially uneasy, which was not missed by his wife or Annie.

But get through the difficult lunch they did, reds and whites helping lull their angst. The absence of Francesca loomed large and they realised it was going to take a while for all of them to get used to it.

"She was such a life force," Jay kicked the conversation off. "Heronsford is so much the poorer for her loss."

"You're so right there, so right. It will never be the same," said Patrick.

"But we cannot allow it to colour our view of the village," said Eliza. "We will pick up again in time and we will have fun again," she paused, "somehow." Her expression did not endorse her words.

"Time heals all," said Katie.

"Time will certainly not heal this. The reminder of Francesca's terrible end stands in the village for all to see whenever they go that way out of the village."

Taken aback by Jay's abrupt tone, Katie's eyes teared up, but she managed to stop herself crying.

Since Francesca's death and a disappointingly small order from the large chain store, Jay's demeanour had once again become tense and now a kind of cynicism and anger had replaced his earlier despondency.

Hamish caught Eliza's eye and for a moment they were united in mutual annoyance with Jay for his crude rebuke, and at Katie for the innocuous platitude trotted out without thought. Eliza sometimes wished Jay possessed half the sensitivity Hamish had.

At the end of the meal, while the women were waiting in the dry for the men to hail enough taxis for the entire party, Annie suddenly said, "I saw a man going into Francesca's cottage that evening."

"My God, Mother! Why ever didn't you say so earlier? Who was it and what time?" Eliza's voice had risen.

"It was late. I'd been supping with Pam and we'd sat up playing chess. I couldn't say for certain who it was. I only saw the back of him. Francesca was welcoming him in."

"This puts a whole new slant on things, Mum. It means it's highly likely poor Francesca was murdered. Did you tell the police?"

"As it happens, I did, darling. But they found no sign of arson or any deliberate act. Francesca was found in her bed, remember."

"Well, now we know, she must have been murdered. There can be no doubt."

Stella looked dumbstruck.

When the men returned, no-one said anything about what Annie had said but a new distrust hung over the group as the women spent the rest of the journey wondering about which man Annie had seen. Annie was fairly certain who it had been, but being a great believer in fairness, since she had not seen the face of Francesca's visitor, she was not prepared to put anyone's name forward.

Hamish and Katie returned to Wood Farm feeling miserable. Katie Nicholson's deepest need was to be surrounded by family and friends; her deepest fear loneliness. In spite of her bubbly demeanour, death always played on her uneasy mind more than it should and Francesca's funeral brought this to the fore of it.

Ever since her parents had died, as children often do, she had felt a kind of guilt that she had been in some way responsible, and had been haunted by their absence. Since then and following the loss of both her grandparents, she sometimes felt an irrational fear that everyone she loved died.

The two recent deaths in the village had brought back the dread she had held in the pit of her stomach as a child. She became quietly terrified that she might now lose Hamish and more and more convinced that he was unhappy with her. The problem was that the more she felt like this, the more Hamish felt suffocated by her incessant new insecurity, jealousy of other women and nervousness that affected her usually relaxed attitude. To counteract this, she was drinking more and more, and her husband was beginning to think she was turning into a full-blown alcoholic.

He knew that she had always felt this fear of losing those she loved, and he did his best to understand why. But Hamish had a relatively straightforward upbringing and a happy childhood, and sympathetic though he might have been, he struggled to comprehend Katie's new nervousness. He could not begin to imagine why these deaths of friends could so affect his wife as to bring out this neediness in her. He carried on as best he could, but with things at the brewery going from bad to worse, and as the prospect of finding a new job locally grew dimmer by the day, he was finding life at Wood Farm becoming a strain.

His son was rude and indifferent, his daughter in some world of her own, the house a mess and getting messier. But more than anything else, more often than not he would return from work to find Katie on the way to finishing a bottle of red wine.

Annie's preference for medium heels was gradually being replaced by the need for flatter ones as her back pain was becoming more constant. Without saying anything to anyone, in August she had made another appointment with Edward Gordon. This time he had asked whether she had weighed herself lately. Dismissing scales as a silly vanity, Annie had to agree that her appetite had not been what it usually was, but that she was certain the hot weather was to blame. Dr Gordon had asked her to stand on the large surgery scales.

"This is quite unnecessary, Edward. I'm just not very hungry at the moment, but I'm sure once we get to autumn my appetite will pep up again."

The scales showed her at ten stone, three pounds. This was a drop from her usual ten and three-quarter stones. He prescribed a stronger painkiller for her back pain and asked her to make another appointment in a fortnight.

Two weeks later, Annie had arrived at the village surgery for her follow-up appointment with the doctor. She had sat in the surgery waiting room flipping through an ancient, well-eared *National Geographic* magazine. After a time, Dr Gordon had popped his head round the waiting room door, "Anne Berkeley?"

Annie had got up and walked stiffly after him into his consulting room. She had sat on a varnished beech chair with a plastic seat beside his desk.

He had smiled. "Well, Annie, tell me how the back has been? Not too good by the look of it."

"To be honest, Edward, the pills don't seem to be helping a lot. It just won't go away, and I am getting a bit fed up with it."

"I'm sure you are." He had consulted Annie's notes on the screen in front of him.

"Would you be able to lie down and allow me to have a feel of your tummy?" He had gestured at the examination table. "Just lift your blouse and undo the top of your trousers."

He had helped her climb onto the couch that was covered with a roll of white paper. She had lain down and lifted her bright blue tunic. Doctor Gordon had felt her stomach carefully, pressing it here and there to see whether she flinched or whether there was any swelling. He had then looked at her eyes through a scope with a light and said, "Annie, I am going to take some blood tests. Hope you're not squeamish?"

"I think you may be making more of this than necessary," said Annie, "but I know you're being thorough and covering for every possibility. And me squeamish?" She had happily rolled up her sleeve while he had found a suitable syringe.

"Just clench your hand a few times and then relax."

The only good news the Armstrongs received in this dismal period was that Juliet had obtained good enough grades to get into Bristol University, where she would start in September. When Eliza and Jay spoke to her in Australia, she sounded elated. They didn't tell her about Francesca's death as they didn't see the point in worrying her when she was clearly loving her time away.

17

23 SEPTEMBER

To her parents' delight, Juliet returned from Australia. She was due to start at Bristol University the following week.

Eliza knew she'd had her engagement ring on at supper. She was certain she had left it in the old teacup on the windowsill above the kitchen sink as she always did when washing-up.

They had invited Patrick and Sinead on the Sunday. All the family had been present including Juliet, who, as Holly pointed out, had been incredibly lucky to have escaped what had turned out to be the most awful Heronsford summer ever.

Everyone had helped load the dishwasher and bring the plates and cutlery from the table. After Patrick and Sinead had left at about 10.15pm and Eliza had finished up the pots and pans in the sink, she reached for the cup and felt for her engagement ring. It was missing.

The tragic deaths of the two young women hung over the village like a shroud that affected everyone. Gossip was rife.

More than anyone, Sinead was badly disturbed. The intermittent nightmares she had suffered following the death of her mother had increased to a terrifying nightly occurrence. The child looked thin, drawn and miserable, and Patrick was at his wit's end to know how to help her.

Although they were now living in Cambridge, they were still officially resident in Heronsford, so they went to see Dr Gordon. He suggested they should both see a grief counsellor, but Patrick decided against the idea as he felt he was beginning to deal with the death himself.

For Sinead he thought it could be a great benefit and she started regularly seeing a woman in Cambridge once a week to talk over the tragedy of losing her mother. Now she had a double grief to deal with and was a mixed-up, confused child who was often sick, sometimes unable to eat and altogether in a bad way.

On top of this, the poor child had to deal with starting at a new school, but Holly was being a staunch friend and as understanding as she could be. Eliza still invited Sinead to stay often, a simple arrangement as she picked Holly up from the station daily and Sinead simply came with her on the train.

Juliet had so much stuff to take with her to university that Eliza drove her down to Bristol, the car filled to the gunnels. It took her quite a while to help her get her things set up in her digs and she decided to stay the night at a cheap hotel. There was no Jay to worry about as he had gone on Bob's annual trip to Scotland.

The wide salmon-rich River Tay borders the park of Scone Palace. Here, large numbers of Atlantic salmon migrate from the Norwegian Sea or the waters around Greenland on their migration to lay their eggs in their own birthplace in the gravel on the bottom of the cold fresh water river.

Every year Bob McKenzie booked eight bedrooms for ten days. Jay and Hamish were generally two of the all-male company. The men were a mixture of friends of Bob's and businessmen involved in estate management or agencies that Bob was either negotiating with for mergers, takeovers or with whom he had some monetary reason to flirt.

Usually each man paid for his hotel room while Bob paid the flights and the extras involved such as days shooting, stalking and fishing, none of which were cheap. This year, to Jay's embarrassment, Bob had insisted on paying for everything. Hamish had paid for his hotel room, but they still felt in debt to Bob for the largesse he lavished on them.

On Friday, 14 September, the eight men took a plane from Stansted Airport to Edinburgh. When they arrived, Bob had hired three Land Rovers to drive up to Scone. The party would keep these for use during their stay. Some days some of the men would fly fish from boats with outboard motors, others would spin from the shore while the rest who had certificates to prove they were capable shots, would stalk deer or drive up to Forneth Moor to shoot grouse where Bob had paid for four days' shooting.

When in Scotland, Bob loved to flaunt his surname as though it would somehow give him some exclusive advantage. In fact, the few remaining drops of Scottish blood in his heritage had long become so diluted to be meaningless.

Hamish, as his name suggests, was a true Scotsman who had been born in Stirlingshire. Most of his childhood had been spent out of doors and he had been imbued with a love for the countryside. He felt very at home here and was glad to get away from the chaos of home and his lacklustre employers. He enjoyed the company of men and found Bob funny, willing to try new things, extremely generous and good company.

Jay did too, but found it much harder being, as he quietly told Hamish, in the man's debt. The reality was that part of him secretly disliked Bob. The only person who knew it was Eliza, who understood the root cause of his antipathy to the man. Jay would never have admitted it and may not have even known himself, but he was in fact jealous of Bob. It annoyed him that Bob didn't "get" that other men don't always enjoy being helped and paid for by another.

Jay didn't like activities that he declined to call "sports" as he disliked the thought of killing animals for the sake of killing. He could not reconcile himself to the idea of setting out to deliberately kill what he considered harmless prey.

He did not extend these feelings towards fish though and was mad about fishing, which he did every day during the stay. Some days in the mornings or afternoons while the others were shooting or deer stalking, he would drive up to the peaks in the north of Perthshire and take long hikes across the hills. He enjoyed these solitary hours, walking on beautiful, remote mountains, and felt freer than he had for some time. Although he loved his family, recently he had felt hemmed in, trapped. If he had only realised it, he would have understood that these feelings were a reaction to the nervous tension he had experienced recently.

On Monday morning, sluggish fleecy clouds barely moved in a pallid sky and the day was unusually still. No breeze ruffled the grasses and heathers on the hills. September is a wet month in Scotland, and they had all come prepared for the worst. The men were grateful for today's break in the weather since, in spite of their waterproofs, waxed jackets and Barbour hats, they'd had to admit the previous two days' fishing had been a bit spoilt by the rain that had fallen steadily most of the time.

They all had a huge early breakfast that started with porridge followed by an egg, mushrooms, tomatoes, beans, black pudding, bacon, a potato scone and toast. Some went shooting, others fishing. Clad in warm camouflage jackets, khaki trousers and heavy waterproof hiking boots, Bob, Hamish and a partner of an estate management agency that Bob had his eye on to take over, drove one of the Land Rovers to take part in a grouse shoot.

That day Jay decided to walk in the morning and fish later. He drove one of the Land Rovers west for about fifty minutes until he came to a loch. Remote, the place was deserted when he parked up and set off to walk a series of wild hills and crags high above sea level.

For about two hours, he walked along a track beside the entire length of the water. He turned right to walk up toward a high bleak hill. Passing through pine trees, the scent pervaded his senses. Stopping occasionally to take photographs with his smartphone, he forded a couple of burns with small waterfalls. Every so often he would pause to take a few breathers along the way and to look down at the great views back down the loch. As he climbed higher, his pace slowed and when he got three quarters of the way up, he stopped. Sitting down on a fallen pine, he caught his breath. He pulled an apple from his pocket. Crunching on it was the only sound he could hear.

Conscious of the strong air and the solitude, he stared down at the steel sheet of water below. There was something about the scene that, for a reason, he could not explain to himself, he found unnerving.

He sat as still as the landscape until, cutting through the silence, a large bird flew into his view, flying slowly at a moderate height over the loch's surface. Jay's heart raced.

The closer it got, the larger it seemed, its wingspan measuring almost two metres. He could not quite believe what he was witnessing. Its outspread wings tipped at their ends like a woman's open hand with bony fingers and sharp fingernails. Its tail feathers were equally distinctly spread. The spectacular black, white and grey bird was something he had never seen before. It wasn't an eagle, but its size was similar to one.

He watched with fascination as the bird slowed to a hover, arced its wings before half folding them and tipped its body forward to become an arrowhead travelling fast at the water. As it neared the loch, it swung forward its powerful legs with their massive talons into a perfectly choreographed position before hitting. There was a huge splash as it struck, went half under the water and came out, a big fish struggling in its fatal grip.

For a moment, the great bird looked like the angel of death, its wings raised high in the air before it regained momentum, lifted off and heaved the flailing pike out of the water. It flew up and away over the top of the hill, the fish still flapping.

Too mesmerised to remember to take photographs, Jay guessed it was an osprey that, with man's help, were re-establishing themselves in Scotland. He decided that later he would check them out on his computer.

Soundless again, the water gradually stilled. As Jay watched the decreasing traces of circles spread gently out from the spot where the bird had fished, he gaped in amazement as something slowly emerged from within them. Gradually breaking the surface of the grey water, a head appeared with long strands of red hair drifting like seaweed around it in the water. A body emerged after it. The figure was face up. Horrified, Jay turned his head away. Rubbing his shocked eyes, he blinked hard a few times. When he turned back to look again, it had gone. He got up and walked back down the hill, peering at the place on the loch all the while. The body had gone but the image would not leave his mind.

Desperate, he walked back to the Land Rover with the picture of a dead female that refused to leave his thoughts. Coming through the pinewood beyond which lay the car park, he glimpsed a flash of orange and heard the roar of an engine that made his neck prickle.

Someone was coming into the car park. He hoped they wouldn't be sitting in their car enjoying the view because he desperately craved a bit of privacy in the shelter of Bob's anonymous hired Land Rover.

And sure enough, there was a Ford Mustang parked up. He'd have known that engine noise anywhere. A man was squatting by the side of it looking a bit ticked off. "Ah, mate, you haven't got a jack, have you? Tyre's flat and I can't seem to make ours work–"

To the man's amazement, clearly distressed, Jay gave him a shocked look, jumped into the Land Rover and sped off, tears streaming down his face. A few miles later, he pulled into a trackway, stopped the Land Rover and cried his heart out.

18

LATE OCTOBER

Once Holly had been back at school for six weeks, Eliza took the last week of October off to get away on her own.

She had borrowed some money from her mother and booked a hotel in the Yorkshire Dales to, as she put it, "come up with some inspiration for new designs." It was actually because she was nearing the end of her tether with her husband.

When she returned on Sunday twenty-eighth, she looked healthier, happier and more relaxed than she had for ages. What no-one knew was that someone had joined her for a couple of days, and this had given Eliza her sparkle back.

The day after her return, Eliza went over to the barn for a cup of coffee with her mother. To Annie's great relief, her daughter seemed happy again, a thing she had not seen for a time. She was not immune to the renewed vivacity in her daughter and had a good idea why it had returned. Eliza told Annie about her holiday and showed her some striking photographs she had taken on her iPad. Annie was impressed.

"Some of them look like paintings. To add to your many talents, you are an excellent photographer, Eliza. You should do more."

Annie felt the worst of her doubts were over, for the moment anyway. Eliza seemed stronger than she had proved earlier in the year, and there was hope that she still might make the marriage work.

"Had any further thoughts on who the man you saw going into Smith's Cottage may have been, Mum?"

"I think of little else. But I really don't feel able to identify him. I know how unreliable eyewitnesses can be."

"Whoever is this murderer? Do you think they also might have killed Louise?"

"I think it is highly possible."

"But why, why, why?"

"Perhaps whoever killed Louise discovered Francesca knew something they did not want spread about?"

"Trouble is, we're no nearer catching whoever it is."

"They will trip themselves up in the end. Murderers usually do."

Eliza shrugged in mock despair. "Well, back to the grindstone... I'd better get on, Mum. Thanks for the coffee."

"Before you go, darling, can I ask you to look after Mildred for three nights? I'm off to stay with Helen on Tuesday."

"Of course, I will, but are you sure you should go, Mum? You seem to be in quite a bit of pain still. Another visit to Edward for you, I think. Wouldn't it be wiser to put it off until they can get this wretched arthritis under better control?"

"Oh, I'm okay. The pills do work when I remember to take them. I'm just getting so forgetful these days. Besides, I haven't seen Helen for ages and I miss her."

"Mum, please don't do too much when you get there. Promise?"

"Promises and pie-crust... honestly, darling, I don't intend to. I'll be back on Thursday."

"Lunch on Sunday as usual, then?"

"I shall look forward."

30 October

Annie's oldest and dearest female friend lived in Bloomsbury. They had been close friends since she and Helen had started out in London as young postgraduates studying for their diplomas in bar practice at Gray's Inn in London.

They had shared a flat for a few years. Together they had taken their bar exams, been called to the bar and shared their first year's experiences of criminal cases with 5am starts, trains to places they would never have otherwise visited, vending machine lunches, interminable waiting and clients who usually offered no thanks for their help. They learnt the hard way the amount of work that went into representing those charged with criminal offences. It had meant being psychiatrist, counsellor, social worker, mother and other things as well. They had to acquire the ability to identify mental health problems, physical and mental abuse and addictions to alcohol or drugs.

Together they had gone through trials they won and lost and had to grow thick skins to deal with disappointments. Losing a case was not a thing they were able to dwell on since their lives were too busy for that. The moment one case was over, it was straight on to reading up on the next one. They had barely had time for private lives outside and tended towards sticking with their own kind.

Waiting on the platform for the 11.09am London train from Heronsford, Annie looked along it to see Stella standing further up. She called her and when Stella heard her name, she looked down the platform to see the little woman dressed in a bright green trouser suit, a multi-coloured scarf around her neck, black suede slip-on trainers with thick white soles and a walking stick. Hunched and clutching a walking stick, Annie B. looked to be in some pain. Stella walked back up to her side.

"How nice to see you, Annie."

"You too, Stella. You look very smart. Where are you off to?"

"And so do you. Love the suit. Me, I'm just up for the day to see some friends for lunch in Knightsbridge, then do a bit of shopping. And you?"

"Well, I also have a lunch planned with old friends, but that is on Wednesday. I am staying for three nights with a girlfriend who I seem to have known forever. I have a few other things to do while I'm in the great metrop."

When the train pulled in, Stella could see just how stiff Annie B. was and felt sorry for the older woman. "You are clearly in pain. Is it the back?"

"It is. Wretched nuisance, but I suppose at my age I've got to expect a few things to go wrong."

"Do you have to go to London? Might it be better to go another day when you are feeling better?"

"I'm sure it would, but the plans are made now and it's too late to alter them. Anyway, I shall enjoy it when I get there."

When Annie reached down to lift her case, without hesitation Stella picked it up and helped her onto the train. They chose opposite window seats with a table in between them.

"What should I have done without you being here?"

Stella laughed. "I think you would have been fine. Someone would have helped you. It's good you have wheels on the suitcase, not so good for you to have to carry it."

Although she had never had any proper conversation with the beautiful but edgy young woman, Stella had never given Annie any reason to dislike her. Now she could see she was a kind person.

She recalled the dreadful incident at the fête when the poor young woman had found her little dog drowned. A deplorable business. Annie wondered whether Stella had come any nearer to the truth of who or what was behind it. She decided she'd wait until they had broken a little more ice before asking her. As they talked, Annie could feel her begin to relax and by the end of the journey, there was little they hadn't covered.

After they arrived at Liverpool Street station, they shared a taxi to drop Annie off in Bloomsbury then to take Stella on to the Knights-bridge restaurant where she was meeting a couple of modelling friends. When Stella offered to pay for the taxi, Annie wouldn't hear of it.

"In the old days, I used to bus everywhere – it's much the nicest way to travel you know, but this time I shall jolly well take taxis. No question that I shall pay my way." When she reached her friend's mews house, Stella asked the taxi to wait while she carried Annie B.'s suitcase to the door. A new bond had been forged between them, and Annie gave her a hug goodbye.

"Stay strong, Stella." She left her new pal feeling very motherly towards her, and concerned about the young woman. They agreed to meet again soon.

Annie and Helen almost fell into each other's arms. They embraced, holding close to one another for a few seconds, then spent the rest of the day chattering and catching up and eating and playing chess.

The following day, Annie had arranged a reunion lunch with twelve old friends from her days at the bar, that included Helen. For what was a meaningful meal for her, she had chosen to have it in the magnificence of the Great Hall at Lincoln's Inn where she had been a barrister. Looking on from the vast "Justice" mural, both Moses and Muhammad watched the five men and eight women on chairs uphol-stered in red leather around the table. Portraits of ancient and more recent red-robed lawgivers hung on sixty-foot high walls with cathe-dral-like arched stone windows above oak panels.

From her place in the middle of one side of the long table, Annie stood up and announced that, more than a reunion, this was to cele-brate her forthcoming seventy-fifth birthday.

"When's your birthday?" someone asked.

"In March," said Annie to much laughter. "But, you see, once I had the idea, I simply had to get on with it. Never was much good at patience. And by the way, the food and drink are on me."

There were rafts of protest, until she stood up. "None of you have any idea of just how happy this is making me. To have you all here is worth a million pounds to me, so now, my learned friends, I respectfully put it to you to pipe down, shut up and let a determined old crock have her way." She raised her glass, "Seriously, here's to you. Thank you so much for being here. I love you all."

They cheered her and told her they loved her too and reminisced and ate and drank champagne and reminisced and ate and drank some more champagne, then a cake was brought forward with a lit candle in the middle to be placed ceremoniously in front of Annie. The company sang *Happy Birthday*, one of the men adding in basso profundo, "in March" to the lyric.

Although the rules of the Great Hall are that lunch finishes by 2.30pm, one of the men at lunch was a high court judge. He, at Annie's request, had a word with the Treasurer to pass it down to those who managed the dining hall that their lunch could be extended until 4pm.

By that time, full of alcohol, food and pain killers, Annie felt extremely tired and Helen had to assist her into a taxi, help her back to Bloomsbury and pour her into bed for a long rest before supper.

But whatever the consequences, she considered it to have been more than well worth it. She had delighted in what she called "a joyful experience". Saying goodbye to the old friends was a wrench, but they, who had also much enjoyed themselves, all swore to make it their business to see her again before long.

Annie had accumulated a lot of money over the years. This was largely for two reasons. The first was that as a barrister she had earned extremely well. The second was that the salary had never been the point. Her desire to work as she had done had never been driven either by a craving for influence, authority or for money. Lacking attraction for money as she did, meant that she had rarely spent it. She'd had no interest in buying especial cars or a grander house or any of the usual things that people enjoy who have money. Her one luxury would have been to travel far and wide with her family to many exotic places. That, it had seemed to her, would have been the best way to spend some of that money and would have been educational for Eliza when she was growing up. But she had never had long enough holidays to take more than a week at a time, so they had tended not to go further than Europe, although they had been to St Petersburg as well as Jordan.

Much of the reading and thinking had been done at home, but her job had meant working six days a week including evenings, only taking time off on weekend afternoons. That had been until she had retired early and come home to be with Robin and her daughter.

Seeing how exhausted the pain was making her friend, Helen persuaded Annie to rest the day following the lunch. Annie gratefully postponed her planned meeting and lunch with Hugh Dunlop, another old friend who happened to be her solicitor, until the following day.

She agreed to stay an extra night.

It took eleven hours sleep to refresh Annie, who woke up at 10.30am on Thursday morning and spent another lovely day with her dear friend in which they did little except eat and play chess and Scrabble.

After her morning meeting and lunch with Hugh on Friday, she caught a train back to Heronsford. Much as she had enjoyed herself, she felt enervated and was glad to get back home. Mildred gave her the usual tremendous welcome.

19

3–5 NOVEMBER

The week in London had taken its toll on her and on Saturday, Annie did little except walk Mildred after breakfast as usual and sit at her bureau to write a few letters. The rest of the day she read her book, only nipping out once to deliver a letter.

When she arrived at the farm on Sunday in time for lunch, she was greatly disappointed to find that the newly happy couple had also invited the Ryans, the McKenzies and the Nicholsons, as well as Pam Sowerby. Rose was there to help with the food and wash-up. Annie had really been hoping to have a quiet lunch with just the family, but Eliza and Jay didn't realise just how much the pain from her back and stomach were grinding her down.

Eliza was back on form and in the mood for entertaining. They produced a huge leg of lamb followed by a bread and butter pudding.

Eliza noticed how little her mother ate, along with the fact that she was clearly losing weight. Her face looked different too. She was a slightly different colour than usual. Something was obviously wrong. Eliza said nothing so as not to embarrass her, but decided that tomorrow morning she would make an urgent appointment with Dr Gordon and, if necessary, drag her mother along to see him. The pain she was in was not right and there must be something the doctor could do.

Annie made her excuses almost the moment lunch was over, and was back in her bed falling asleep by 2.30pm. Mildred, as always, was happy to join her. When she woke an hour and a half later, she made herself get up and go through to the sitting room.

Opening the French doors to the last weak rays of the autumn sun that was sinking fast, Annie fixed herself an extra-large gin and tonic and took it out to her patio. She had brought a cushion out with her and put it behind her as she sat down on the weather bleached bench. Mildred trotted after her and sat on her foot until Annie gave in and helped her onto her lap. The little dog promptly fell asleep again.

Vivid stripes of corals, peaches, pinks, greys and pale blues painted the broad sky over the dark woods beyond the deepening field. A still, beautiful landscape of colour. *Our view*, she thought.

Wrapped in memories, she thought about all the people she loved and had loved. Her thoughts wandered to and fro through her life. She felt sad about missing the many places she had failed to visit, the many old friends she had failed to keep up with, the times when she had been thoughtless, unfair or unkind. She knew it was too late now. As the last traces of the sun gave way to a rich dark blue, she sat on under the stars. She thought about the beauty of that simple scene and that how, by just gazing at it, it had comforted her so many times.

She hadn't looked after her husband as well as she should have because her work had been too important to her. She hadn't said goodbye to him properly before he died. She recalled how she had allowed herself to be irritated when, instead of fixing the broken door handle in the kitchen or mowing the too long grass, he had stood by the barbed wire fence painting the view she had just been watching. Robin had painted so many local landscapes but "their view", as they had called it, he had rendered over and over again because he so loved it. She wondered whether she had failed to tell Robin enough how much she had really loved him.

Melancholy and regrets rippled through her mind until something made her glance up. Low against the navy sky, the farmyard resident barn owl set off on his or her nightly hunt. Annie gasped with pleasure as she watched the spectral bird's slow soundless flight over her garden, gliding on its silent passage to sail over the fields before disappearing from view. She shuddered. It was getting cold. From her lap, Mildred felt the movement, looked up at her mistress and snuffled. The dog remembered her supper and by grinning, panting and snorting, made it obvious what she wanted. The old pragmatist sighed. She tickled Mildred behind the ears before carefully tipping the little dog onto the ground. Together, they went indoors.

Annie took double her usual dose of painkillers, fed Mildred then dragged the chair at her bureau over to the French windows and placed it in front of them. Her back and her stomach still ached but she walked to the corner of her sitting room. She removed her cello from its hard case before lifting it and the bow. With much difficulty, the stooped old lady carried them slowly across to the chair. She placed the cello in position and sat down facing the dark beyond. She couldn't see it, but she imagined the view was still visible.

Annie Berkeley closed her eyes and played. The intense poignancy of "The Swan" filled the high rafters of the room as she played the piece with more feeling than ever before. As she played it, she could hear the rippling piano accompaniment in her head. Enthralled, she played it again. She followed it with the Elgar concerto first movement, but it wasn't the same and one last time she played the Saint-Saëns.

20

5 NOVEMBER

Following a bad night, on Monday morning Eliza, still in her dressing gown, drove Holly to the station to catch the school train. She'd had some horrible nightmares and felt entirely unrefreshed by what little sleep she had managed.

When she got home, she went straight upstairs to run a bath. Once it was half full, she scattered a few drops of her treasured bath oil in the water. Francesca had given it to her for her birthday and she rarely used it. She couldn't bear the thought of the bottle becoming empty. While there was still some in the bottle, she could feel a little piece of her friend remained.

She draped her dressing gown and nightdress on the chair next to the bath and stepped into the steaming bathwater. She closed her eyes and sighed. For a while she relished the luxury of having some time to herself. Jay was working in the office and fortunately there was nothing she had to do today. She felt exhausted. Opening her eyes again, she watched the slow drip of the cold tap splash into the bathwater, and the nightmares came back into her mind. The feeling of unease that she had felt most of the night lingered and she wondered why this uncomfortable sensation had descended on her now. After all, things were hopefully looking up, although John Spencer still hadn't confirmed their autumn order.

She decided that last night's late supper of goat's cheese and spinach tart was the probable cause of her bad night and the feeling that something was wrong. She recalled a story about Salvador Dali eating an oozing, overripe Camembert before painting "The Persistence of Memory" where in a bleak, nightmarish landscape, melting stopwatches represented the cheese.

Still lying in the bath, she heard the doorbell go. There was no-one in the house to answer. She presumed it was the postman. One more ring then the bell was silent. Probably trying to deliver a parcel. He'd leave a card if so, which meant she'd have to go to the post office in Broxton to collect it later. She thought about her mother who hadn't been herself yesterday. Eliza's heart ached for her. She would try to persuade her to see Dr Gordon later.

Aware of what an awful night his wife had had, Jay suggested that she should take herself back to bed for the morning. He had assured her there was nothing pressing workwise.

Eliza lay a while longer in the bath but the water was growing cold and she made herself get out, dry and get dressed. She dawdled over this. A strange reluctance to face the day hampered her movements. However silly it was, she didn't seem to be able to shake the sensation. She would listen to Jay and go back to bed for an hour or so. All she needed was some sleep.

Foot down on the accelerator, Hamish drove too fast through Heronsford before joining a main road that led to the A11 for Bury St Edmunds. He was late for work again that morning but this time much later than usual. He hadn't left until after 10am. Today was the day he was making some big changes to his life. Things could only get better now. He glanced at his shoes on the pedals and realised he was still wearing the grubby trainers he'd been out in earlier. Should he go back and get the lace-ups he usually wore for work? *No,* he thought with certainty, *I won't. I've got no reason to care anymore.*

That same morning at about 9.30am, Annie took Mildred for their daily morning walk. It was the sort of day when a pale light dominates the landscape, making the far distance surprisingly clear and you notice things you rarely have before.

Dressed in her favourite bright blue blouse and trousers, a blue and red cotton paisley hip-length jacket and navy ankle boots with red laces, with her new walking stick in hand, she and Mildred set out across the field. She was bent and slow because of the pain, but she would not allow it to prevent Mildred's daily constitutional, as she called it. When Jock and Eeyore saw her, they trotted over, expectant as ever. As always, she took a couple of carrots out of her pocket and fed the animals, patting, stroking and murmuring to them while they munched.

She walked on to the gate that led to a small wooden bridge across the river, built by Eliza's ancestors in Victorian times. She crossed the bridge, Mildred trotting behind her.

On the far side a spindle bush was in full fruit, its leaves turning from green to hues of red and orange. Annie stopped to gaze at the strange, extraordinary berries as vibrant as any of her favourite outfits, glorious deep pink opening to vivid orange seeds. Being a gardener, she knew it was a Euonymus and was aware of the plant's poisonous properties. She recalled showing the enticing fruit to little Eliza and warning her never to try to eat the berries. She had pointed out the irony to her daughter that the plant dresses to please, but pleases to harm, even to kill.

A flock of wild geese bayed like crazed hounds as they flew low overhead. Annie walked along the path that led into Rooks Wood. It was only a path because ponies, dogs, humans, badgers, deer and muntjac had trodden down the grass so many times that long ago the ground had become bare.

The music of *Madam Butterfly* played in her head as she went into the wood. Fatigue began to catch up with her. Walking slowly, Annie stopped often to rest. She had come to terms with what today held in store and that there was nothing she could do now to change it.

Little light entered the wood here and the trees grew thick and close. Taught as a child never to look down but always to look up, she paused at a place where the path narrowed. Tipping her head back to gaze up at the tall treetops, she searched for chinks of sky. The great circumferences of the older sycamores trapped her attention with their silvery grey and brown bark cracked and peeling. She studied the ash trees with their deep green deeply fissured ridges and the vertical plates on the alders looked as though a sculptor had slapped long pieces of rough brown clay on their trunks. She looked closely for lichens, mosses and minute insects. She breathed in the delicious smell of damp woodland. She listened to the raucous shrieks of the rooks and crows in the treetops. She contemplated the huge diversity of nature within this little wood and thought about how vast the differences must be in the galaxy. She thought about how long the galaxy had existed and remembered reading recently that Madagascar was ninety million years old.

The last few lines of *The Road Less Taken* came to her. "Two roads diverged in a wood and I – I took the one less travelled by, and that has made all the difference."

A terrible searing pain ran through her as the vicious object smashed against her head. Reeling sideways, she half turned for a moment to see the face of her attacker before the second blow rained down. She didn't feel the third when her skull cracked open and was already gone by the time the fourth and the fifth strikes hit. Annie B.'s lifeless body lay in a distorted heap on the woodland floor. Rooks Wood watched her killer creep away. Crows screamed and smaller birds whistled in alarm. The place fell silent but for the high, outlandish whines of the little dog whimpering at her mistress's side.

At about ten thirty, deciding fresh air might help clear her bleary head, Hamish's wife Katie took Homer for a walk. She ambled to the bottom of their garden to go through the little wooden gate they had put in that led to a path through Long Wood.

She was unsurprised when the dog disappeared since it was typical of the crazy animal. He went wherever his nose took him. This time though, he was an unusually long time gone. Katie set off in the direction he'd headed, whistling and calling his name. There were rabbits in the wood. It wouldn't be unusual to discover he'd put one up and was giving chase.

At the end of Long Wood, she stepped out onto the edge of the ploughed field. Checking all directions, she soon spotted Homer on the other side running into Rooks Wood on the Armstrongs' land. She knew they wouldn't mind if she followed him, which she did with a struggle since walking round the edge of the field, her boots quickly became heavy with mud. When she reached the farm track along the edge of the field, she made quicker headway. Tired of shouting, Katie gave up and simply followed the direction the dog had taken. She followed the perimeter of the wood until she found the faint trace of a narrow track probably made by deer or badgers where she had seen Homer disappear.

She crossed a ditch and pushed through an overgrown hedgerow. There seemed to be no other way in and as she struggled through the thicket, stray brambles reached for her, snagging her coat, trousers and hair. She pulled herself free, thinking, *wish I'd never followed that damn dog*. Once she was into the wood, she took a while to find a path leading deeper into it.

Excited barks sounded ahead of her. She caught a glimpse of

Homer's black and white body through the trees. Katie yelled his name and this time the dog came back to her. He rushed up to her, wagging his tail in an agitated frenzy. Panting with his tongue hanging out, he kept looking from Katie and back to where he had come from. To her surprise, Katie realised Homer was trying to tell her something. The dog set off back into the wood and kept stopping to glance back at her. It was as though he was asking her to follow him. She went with him for a short distance until rounding a bend she found him standing over a large blue shape in the undergrowth. To her further surprise, Annie's pug came trotting towards her, wagging her tail in welcome. She bent down to pick up Mildred who was snuffling even more than usual.

"What's up, Mildred? What is it?"

It took a few more yards for her to see what it was; a fallen body with bright blue trousers. Her own legs were reluctant to take her any nearer. Forcing herself forward, she approached. Too terrified to look, she stopped a few yards from the corpse. Even in the darkened gloom of this part of the wood, a quick glance told her what she already knew. Annie B. lay crumpled on the ground, flies buzzing around her. Her body was twisted, her head at a strange right angle in a pool of dark blood, half the skull bashed in, the right eye missing.

Still managing to clutch on to Mildred, Katie backed a few steps away from the scene before the full shock hit. She dropped the little dog as she sank to her knees and stretched out her arms to prevent herself falling. Shuffling her trembling body over to lean against the trunk of a tree, she turned away from the scene.

With shaking hands, she covered her face as she began to cry. Nausea overcame her and she threw up onto the ivy-covered ground. Still barking and sniffing round the corpse, Homer came straight to her when she screamed his name. She put him on his lead. She looked for Mildred, who had returned to the body and was sitting panting beside her dead mistress.

Katie knew she must act. But what should she do? She felt cold, weak and confused. She was unable to think clearly and her hangover was not helping. Then she realised she must go home, call the police, drink a glass of water and when they came, guide them to the body.

Then what? She remembered Eliza. *Oh God,* she thought. *Who would break it to her?* The enormity of what had happened was just beginning to sink in. *What should I do? It's too much to bear.* She sat a while longer staring at the dog. Without Homer, she might not have been found... it didn't bear thinking about. With her right hand still shaking, she groped in the pocket of her Barbour jacket for her phone. He'd know what to do. She called Hamish.

He listened to Katie's rambling, shaking voice and was only just able to make sense of what she was telling him. Taken aback by this incomprehensible event, he rubbed his temples and said, "Let me think for a minute. I need to think. I'll call you straight back, I promise. Don't do anything. Just stay there. You're in shock."

While Hamish collected his thoughts and worked out the best thing to say to his traumatised wife, he realised he must go home to be with her. This had completely ruined his plans. But since it had happened, he must act.

Having had an hour's sleep after her bath, Eliza was dressed and feeling more rested. She was in the kitchen making a shepherd's pie from the left-over lamb roast they'd had the previous day, when, for the third time that morning, the doorbell rang. Eliza opened the front door to see two male policemen. They looked nervous.

The moment she saw them, a horribly unfamiliar but remembered feeling hit her. She felt sick. She knew what they were going to say. Saying nothing herself, she stared at the officers until one of them spoke, "Good morning, madam. Are you Mrs Armstrong?"

She replied automatically. For some reason she felt a heightened sensitivity to the fact that it was starting to spit rain.

"May we come in, please?"

Without a word, she left the door open and walked into the sitting room. Her legs beginning to feel wobbly, she sank onto an armchair. The police stood awkwardly in the room. The plain clothes man in charge introduced himself as Detective Chief Inspector Alan Waterman and the other policeman as a family liaison officer. But all Eliza could hear was a buzzing in her ears.

The younger officer hovered uncomfortably while the more relaxed but stiff detective said, "I'm afraid we have some very bad news, Mrs Armstrong."

Eliza heard herself shout, "It's Mum, isn't it? It's Mum! I know it is!"

"Is Mr Armstrong at home? It would be best if he were present."

She half screamed the words, "Just tell me!"

"I am very sorry, Mrs Armstrong, but it is about your mother. I'm afraid she has been found in what we believe is known as Rooks Wood."

"Is she all right? What's happened? In Rooks?" She half laughed in the man's face.

"Mrs Armstrong, I am very sorry to have to tell you that Mrs Berkeley is deceased."

"Deceased? Deceased? She's dead? She can't be?"

The second policeman came over to Eliza and gently put a hand on her shoulder. "Where might Mr Armstrong be, Eliza? I think he should be here."

Eliza's voice was small. She managed to say, "In the office."

"Are you able to explain where the office is, please?"

"Over there." Eliza gestured in the direction of the yard.

"Shall I, sir?"

"Yes please." The detective stood looking around the room. It was plain how ill at ease he was.

Soon, the other policeman returned with Jay behind him. His face grey and shocked, he rushed to Eliza's side. Dropping to his knees, he wrapped his arms around her and held her. They sobbed together. Eventually Eliza let go of him and leant forward in the chair.

"Was it a heart attack?"

"I'm afraid it is worse than that, Mrs Armstrong. I am very sorry to tell you that it appears Mrs Berkeley was the subject of a brutal attack."

Eliza sat still, her body rigid. "What did you say? What did you say?" She felt nauseous.

Jay, who had by now moved to the arm of the armchair, rose to his feet. He looked furious.

Both policemen stepped nearer the couple. People react in many different ways to the news of violent death and it is impossible to predict how any one person will respond.

Jay glared at the policemen, his fists clenched. "What the bloody hell are you talking about?"

"I really am very sorry to have to tell you, sir, but Mrs Berkeley was killed by a deliberate blunt force trauma to the head."

Eliza had started to ask "How? Where? Why?" when she fell back into the chair and passed out.

Hamish had arrived home by the time the police reached Wood Farm. In spite of her acute distress, Katie had managed to carry Mildred home and to explain the whereabouts of the body to the police. They had bought an Alsatian with them to help sniff out the corpse. They asked Hamish to explain how vehicles could reach the wood. He showed them where the farm track led off the lane near their house to the back of Rook's Wood.

The murder scene was soon discovered. A tent was erected over the body. The scene of crime officer worked alongside the police, locating, collecting, preserving and cataloguing what little evidence there was. While wild animals hadn't yet discovered the corpse, the crows had already taken one of her eyes and, along with blowflies, had found her wounds before the body's discovery. DCI Waterman was studying the ground around a nearby tree.

A young officer who had been posted to wait by the entrance to the wood, shouted, "Pathologist's here, guv! Shall I show her the vic?"

The detective came towards the threesome walking towards the dead body. He introduced himself to the forensic pathologist and her assistant.

"An old girl been whacked."

"Who found her?"

"Local woman walking her dog this morning. The dog sniffed her out."

"Know who she is yet?"

"The woman knew her. Mrs Berkeley from Manor Farm."

"Anne Berkeley, no less! She was a well-known criminal defence barrister. She tended to support the poor and underdogs, usually getting them off. A good woman by all accounts."

The detective felt deeply that someone who had used the law for what they believed were good reasons was worthy of his very best attempt to find who killed her.

"Any weapon found?" the scene of crime officer asked.

"Not yet. We're still searching."

When she arrived, the pathologist was fairly certain that what they politely called "the victim" was lying where she was killed and that no attempt had been made to move her. It looked as though there has been no resistance to the attack and that the woman had been hit with great force from behind, probably falling at once, where the assailant had finished the job with further blows. Nor, it seemed, had anything been taken from the body: her rings, a necklace and a bracelet were present.

The pathologist took samples of the blood spill on the ground, tapings from exposed body surfaces and clothing as well as combing out some head hair. She swabbed the mouth, teeth and genitals. She took scrapings from underneath the fingernails, but her main examination was of the head wounds. To move the body before this had happened would mean placing the head in a separate bag from the body, risking bleeding into the bag that could result in vital evidence going missing. This was a challenging task. It was never easy to establish what weapon had caused such injuries as Annie's.

The first question she needed to establish was whether the timing of injuries coincided with the time of death. She concluded that they fitted with perimortem. Studying the angles of the depressed and linear fractures on the back-right side of the cranium, she established they were consistent with a right-handed aggressor. She searched for obvious remnants of wood or metal but with no luck. The question of what was used to kill the old woman would have to wait until the autopsy.

While this was happening, the area around the murder scene was thoroughly searched. The police tried to work out from whence the killer had come and how they had got there. Was the incident spontaneous or planned? What escape route had the killer taken?

There were no obvious clues to go on. The ground was very dry and although they did find trampled ivy and broken debris on the ground where it looked as though someone had stood close to a broad tree trunk, there were no clues or footprints found on the ground. The trail Katie had left when she had forced her way through the hedgerow could be seen but there were no signs that anyone else had trodden that way to enter the wood. Had the killer followed Annie or waited for her hidden somewhere in the wood? Had they come in from the east side as had Annie, or via the farm track on the west side that lead straight to a well-worn path through the wood? This western path conjoined with the oval one that traced the shape of the copse returning to itself at the east end. This was the one that Annie and other Armstrongs normally used.

In the depths of the wood, police found the remnants of a recently abandoned site where it looked like someone had illegally camped.

They found discarded syringes with traces of heroin and empty food cans nearby. They worked on the theory that Annie may have stumbled upon this person and been killed by them.

However, photos were taken of a place beside a large tree close to the crime scene where it looked as though someone had stood for a while, because the undergrowth was broken and flattened. There were no footprints, or anything found to give any clues as to who it might have been.

So now, they had two possibilities. If a heroin addict had killed her, it is likely they would have made attempts to remove the rings and the bracelet Robin had given her that Annie had always worn. But this had not happened.

Forensics soon worked out that the fire had not been lit for some weeks, traces of insects and bacteria in the cans corroborating this.

"Time of death? Any guesses?" The DI asked the pathologist.

"Judging from the signs of lividity throughout the body and given its temperature and the blood clotting, it was not long ago. Finding her so soon has been an advantage. I would say..." her watch read 1.10pm, "...probably somewhere between 9.30am and 10.30am, nearer 10am. Officially, I'd have to say 9am to 11am."

"Thank you. That's most helpful."

The detective now considered the motive. With nothing obvious stolen and no signs that the body had been interfered with, spontaneous greed was discounted. Jealousy? Hardly. Revenge? Possibly. Sex? No. Hate? Thrill? Perhaps the former, but surely not the latter in so out of the way a place. He considered the old police adage, "find out how a person lived, and you will find out how they died" and wondered whether that could be applied in this strange case of an old lady killed while walking her dog on her grounds.

Shattered by what she heard, Rose Cooper was barely able to respond to Jay when he called. For as long as she could remember, she had adored Annie B. The news would not sink in. After the phone call, she sat at her kitchen table weeping for a long time. A person who drank little alcohol, she pulled out the brandy usually kept for special occasions. Shuddering at the rich, strong taste, she gulped down a glass.

She wished Chris had been at home. She called his mobile asking if he could come home as soon as possible. She could not recall ever feeling as bereft as she did today. The questions went around and around her head. *How dare such a thing happen? How was it possible someone had killed such a wonderful person? Why? Why? Why?*

She drank two more glasses of brandy. She needed to sleep before facing Eliza and the family later.

Within an hour and half, Chris arrived home to find Rose snoring loudly on their bed. He laid down beside her and put a heavy arm over her sleeping body. She stirred and gripped hold of his hand. They cried together.

The phone rang and rang in the Armstrongs' house. Jay was deliberating avoiding answering but it was so persistent that he finally took the call. It was Hamish, who apologised for calling but explained that Katie had found Annie, that he was back at home and that they had Mildred and were happy to keep her for the meantime.

Mildred! They had quite forgotten about the little dog. At least she was cared for and with friends. He thanked Hamish and asked him to pass on his gratitude and sympathy to poor Katie who was apparently still in shock.

Hamish had called the doctor, she had been given a sedative and was sleeping in bed.

Doctor! Sedative! Jay tried to clear his head. In spite of the police suggesting it, he had forgotten to call Dr Gordon. He was about to do so when the doctor appeared at the door. The kindly faced man removed his rain-soaked trilby, bent his head, came into Manor Farm and, giving Jay a small hug, told him how very sorry he was.

He himself had been terribly shocked by the news of his old friend's manner of death. "I've seen Katie Nicholson and she's in a dreadful state. And the police have contacted me too," he told Jay. "They've asked me to send Annie's medical records to the coroner's officer and the pathologist."

Jay had insisted Eliza rested in bed and showed Dr Gordon up to their bedroom. Together, the men sat on the bed beside the distraught woman. The doctor desperately tried to comfort Eliza. He took hold of her hand. "I am so dreadfully sorry to hear about what has happened. I cannot imagine how you must be feeling, Eliza."

She looked at him in misery.

"The only comfort I can offer is to remind you that your mother had only months left to live. Terrible though this is, a quick death like that has saved her what would have been a slow, painful and horrible one."

Silence was all Jay and Eliza could hear. As the doctor's words slowly sank in, they both looked at him in amazement.

The doctor's eyes widened. "Oh, good heavens! You didn't know? She didn't tell you? Oh, good gracious, I had no idea..." his words trailed away, and for a few moments the three of them became soundless sitting statues.

Eliza rubbed her exhausted eyes. Jay ran his hand through his hair again and again. This was too much to take in. What was the man saying?

All Eliza could manage to say was, "What?"

Jay clutched hold of her other hand.

"I presumed, um, I thought, er, I'm so sorry. I assumed she would have told you." The doctor cleared his throat. "Mrs Berkeley was suffering from advanced pancreatic cancer. It was incurable and she knew she had between two and six months to live."

They were both unable to speak. Eliza's head spun with the shock of it all. This couldn't be true. Her mum would have told her. Then she began to laugh. The laughter grew and soon she was cackling hysterically.

Dr Gordon opened his old Gladstone bag.

"Eliza, I am going to give you an injection that will help you deal with this dreadful shock. It will help you relax and sleep and feel a little better."

He rubbed one of her arms with ethanol and injected her with Midazolam. Within five minutes, she was calm again, and in ten she was fast asleep.

"Yes, er, are Mr and Mrs McKenzie in, please?"

The housekeeper showed Hamish into the sitting room. "I believe Mrs McKenzie is in the gymnasium, sir. Mr McKenzie is in his study. I'll fetch him."

"Could you ask them both to come, please? I have some very sad and important news."

"Goodness! Yes, of course, oh dear, I'm so sorry. I shall let Mr McKenzie know straightaway."

Bob strode into the sitting room.

"Hamish! What's all this? Not some prank, I trust? Mrs Hammond said you mentioned something about a death? Not another, surely?"

At that point, Stella ran into the room. Panting slightly, she was wearing trainers and a black leotard with her blonde hair tied in a ponytail.

Hamish suggested they sit down. Then he broke the news. "Thought I should tell you and a few other friends before it gets in the papers or you call Jay and Eliza without knowing."

A dark silence descended on the room. Then Bob said, "Are you sure? Annie B.? But we saw her yesterday. It can't be possible." He fell quiet again. Hamish waited for him to absorb the information. Then he continued, "But why? Why would anyone want to kill a harmless old lady? In such a frightful way? I just can't believe what you're telling me, Hamish. You a hundred per cent certain you've got the facts right?"

"Katie found her, Bob. In Rooks Wood. Head bashed in."

Stella's mouth went dry. She began to shake. Not Annie B. Not her lovely new friend, that sweet, kind-hearted old lady who had given her such good advice when they had met on the train. How was it possible? It was just too, too sad. She was unable to speak. Bob went to her side and put his arm round her.

"Oh Jesus Christ! Oh my God!" he said. "How simply goddam frightful. Why would anyone do such a thing? I mean, who uses that wood apart from the Armstrongs themselves? After all, it is private property. What are the police saying?"

"I don't know any more about it. It only happened this morning. Just wanted to let you both know. Poor Katie's in shock but that's nothing to the way Eliza and the family must be feeling. I must go as I have to collect the kids from school. Others to call too."

"Understood, understood," said Bob. "What a terrible piece of news but good of you to let us know. Jesus Christ! Can't take it in! Give our love to poor old Katie – must have been a goddam awful shock, poor girl."

"Heronsford seems to be cursed."

"It certainly does."

Stella still couldn't speak. She just nodded, tears gently rolling down her cheeks. Hamish left quietly. He had done what had to be done.

Regular contact was made between the pathologist and the DI that continued throughout the murder investigation. For the police, their first tasks were to ascertain motive, opportunity and means. As far as they were concerned, no murder was perfect and people usually do not cover their tracks as well as they think they have done. The vast majority of murderers are known to their victims, although in this case, Annie may have stumbled across some wrongdoing or been the subject of attack for gain.

Jay did not want to leave Eliza's side in case she woke up.

The police had stayed at the farm asking Jay many questions. He was asked where he had been at the time Annie had died. When he said he had been in his office, the police asked for any proof he had to offer. He was able to say he had spoken to Eliza on his phone at about ten when she called him about the doorbell ringing at the house that she couldn't answer because she was in the bath. He told them he had been on his computer making changes to the Eliza Berkeley Designs website. Before long, it became too much for him and, choking with emotion, he broke down in tears.

"I loved her too, you know. I really loved her. She was wonderful and a better mum than I ever had. Today I need to be with my wife. Can't you please come back another time? Just let us have some time to take this all in and be alone. Please."

DCI Waterman nodded solemnly. "You must understand, Mr Armstrong, that a terrible crime has been committed and that it is our duty as officers of the law to find out by whom and for what reason. Until that time, you and your family will be expected to remain on these premises; in other words, no expeditions without our cooperation, okay? The family liaison officer who has been assigned to your case will visit you here again tomorrow. You can ask him all the questions you like. He is there to help you and the family."

"I do understand, of course. Thank you, officers, for all your help, and we'll see you tomorrow."

21

6–8 NOVEMBER

THE DAILY TELEGRAPH

Elderly Lady Barrister Found Bludgeoned To Death

Anne Berkeley, a 74-year-old retired London barrister, has been murdered in what the police called a "despicable and cowardly assault." It happened when Mrs Berkeley was walking her dog in a local wood near her home at Heronsford in Cambridgeshire. Walking her own dog later, a neighbour found Mrs Berkeley beaten to death.

Cambridgeshire Constabulary has launched a murder investigation following Monday morning's discovery. No arrests have been made.

Mrs Berkeley's next of kin, who live in Heronsford, have been informed and a post-mortem is expected to take place later this week.

The detective chief inspector in charge of the case, said, "I want to ask anyone who saw or heard anything suspicious to call police immediately. Did you hear anyone in distress or notice someone in the area who may have looked out of place? Even a fragment of information is beneficial to our investigation. Whoever carried out this brutal attack is dangerous, and it is imperative that we find the person or those responsible for this horrendous offence."

The following day, the police returned to the farm. Still extremely shaken up, Eliza and Jay were questioned for what seemed to them, ages. The senior investigating officers were accompanied by what was turning out to be a sympathetic family liaison officer. He bustled off to make tea for them all and tried to make the interviews as friendly as possible. He did not want the couple alarmed at this stage. When Eliza started to weep again, he sat beside her and said, "You're doing really well, Eliza, really well. You're being a great help and together we'll get whoever did this, don't you worry."

Since Manor Farm was the only house along the no-through road, house-to-house inquiries were ruled out. Instead, among the many things the police wanted to know was who had recently visited the farm. Jay provided them with the names, addresses and numbers of those who had been to lunch on the Sunday; a day that seemed a very long time ago. The police also asked them whether they would object to the whole family giving their fingerprints. The DI had a mobile fingerprinting device, so they wouldn't need to go to the police station. They were reassured it was normal practice and more than likely so that the police could eliminate them from their enquiries.

"As you can see, my daughter isn't home from school yet. Can you leave fingerprinting her until tomorrow, please? We would like time with her alone to explain what happened to her grandmother, about which she will be extremely upset. She spent last night staying with a friend. She's only twelve. Our eldest, Juliet is at Bristol University and has not been here for over a month. If you want hers, you'll have to go to Bristol."

"Yes of course, Mr Armstrong. We just need to rule them out. Thank you for your understanding."

In the lab, the pathologist set to work again. She used a stereoscope to search for remnants of other material such as wood or metal and found some single metal particles, smears and a powder-like deposit on the bone surface. She had taped together the pieces of broken skull and the pattern suggested a heavy blunt instrument with a space between two blunt heads. It was finally concluded that the weapon had been a twelve- to fifteen-inch monkey wrench.

Now the police needed to hunt for it. They had found nothing in Rook's Wood so either someone had kept it or thrown it somewhere, the most likely place being the river.

The police searched the riverbank on the wood side but there was no trace that any human had recently been near. The investigating officer saved the expensive and time-consuming business of the river for later, if they could not find the weapon elsewhere.

The autopsy also revealed that Annie had advanced pancreatic cancer and she would have had only a few months to live. They released the provisional results within a few days of the murder, although the full findings of the inquest would not be available for at least six weeks.

The police had interviewed the McKenzies, the Nicholsons, Patrick Ryan, Pam Sowerby and Rose Cooper, and of course the Armstrongs, in depth, collating their various stories of how the lunch had gone on Sunday.

"It was a nice lunch," Katie had said. Then added with a glance at Hamish, "Even if the lamb was a bit overdone."

Leaping to Eliza's defence, Hamish had countered this with, "I thought it was cooked exactly right. It was a lovely fun lunch, as it always is when Eliza entertains."

Katie had seemed to grit her teeth and look annoyed. The police didn't know that lately she was becoming more certain that her suspicions about her husband were correct. Except that now she had decided Hamish was not having an affair with Stella but with Eliza.

Hamish described Jay as even more anxious than usual. But then, fearing that might have incriminated his friend, he added, "But, you know, the poor guy's got serious business problems, so he's anxious anyway."

"Lovely lunch, it was," Bob had said. "Excellent company apart from Annie who seemed a bit off form. Think she was in some kind of pain, poor old woman. She was definitely limping."

Rose, who had come in to help with the serving and washing-up, commented that everyone seemed happy and that things appeared normal except for Annie. "She left early as I think, unusually for her, she wasn't enjoying herself. Actually, I had been worried about Annie B., sorry, I mean Mrs Berkeley, for some time. She was definitely losing weight and was in quite a bit of pain. But she didn't seem to take it seriously. I did once suggest she went to the doctor but she told me she was fine. It was just a bit of back pain."

Patrick had also mentioned how out of sorts Annie B. had seemed.

They had asked each individual for samples of their fingerprints and DNA to "exclude them from any enquiry into Mrs Berkeley's death".

Stella had hesitated. "It's just... I had my nails done this morning." The detective had smiled kindly and promised it would wash off with soap and water.

The police also asked what they had been wearing at the time. This seemed very strange to those being asked. They wondered why ever the police would want to know that. When he met Hamish and Katie in the pub later that day, Bob exploded, "Bloody goddamned cheek. What the hell do they need to know about the clothes I wore on Sunday for?"

On Tuesday morning, deeply upset by the news of Annie B., excusing herself from lectures, Juliet had caught a train back from Bristol to London and then to Heronsford. She had been determined to be as much a rock to her parents as she could.

Forever grateful to Eliza for her help when Louise had died, Patrick had suggested Holly stayed with him until things sorted themselves out. Sinead empathised strongly with Holly, who had been shaken to the core by Annie B.'s murder. The two girls became interdependent on one another.

Rose had driven Holly to Cambridge in time for school in the morning. Eliza knew Holly wanted to stay at home, but she felt that it would do her no good to hang around brooding and better that she should struggle through school. She hoped Holly would stay away from home as long as possible at the moment.

Hugh Dunlop, Annie's solicitor, was fond of spicy food. On Monday, 5 November, he had taken his wife out to supper in an Indian restaurant near their home in London. They'd had a delicious meal. She a tandoori and he, a pork curry.

Soon after midnight, it had started. His stomach had woken him, suggesting he ran to the bathroom. The ensuing havoc with his system meant he had spent the majority of the night in that room along with symptoms of fever, stomach cramps, nausea and diarrhoea. There was no possibility of his going into the office that day so he lay sleeping most of the day, trying to recover in his bed.

On Wednesday, he'd got up and started to dress for work, but he was so obviously weak and exhausted that his wife had sent him back to bed. So again, he had slept most of the day. Even noise had bothered him so the radio beside his bed remained silent. Having tried a little bread and butter in the evening, it had just exacerbated the problem and he'd crawled back to bed.

Over supper on that same evening, Bob suggested he and Stella should take a long holiday to get away from what had turned into a devastated village.

"We could ask the Nicholsons to join us if you'd like, angel. They'd be as glad to get away as us."

"They have children," said Stella, cynicism icing her words. "And I don't want to go away. We went in August and I don't want to go again."

However hard Bob tried to lay down the law, however intimidating he was, she remained adamant. "I won't go. I want to be here to give Eliza support."

Bob was clearly aggravated. "Eliza doesn't need you, Stella. You're hardly an old friend. You come with me and do as your old man recommends."

It nearly started a major row between them. Stella always did as Bob wanted, but this time she had found courage and was sticking to her guns. She refused to go.

"And you should be here to support Jay," she said with more boldness than she had ever found to speak to her husband before.

On Wednesday morning at 7.30am there was a knock on the door of Manor Farm. Still in his dressing gown, Jay answered it. Four policemen stood on the doorstep with the senior investigating officer, whose face was long and serious. He held up a formal looking piece of paper. It had the royal crest in the centre of the top. He showed it to Jay. A headline ran across the page under the crest: "Warrant to enter and search premises."

He said, "This warrant gives us the right to search this property and to seize any articles we believe to be possible evidence in the killing of Anne Berkeley. May we come in, please?"

Dumbfounded, Jay said, "Can we refuse?"

"I'm afraid you would be breaking the law were you to attempt to do so, Mr Armstrong." No nice DCI and "sir" today.

Jay threw his hands in the air and shook his head. "But my daughter is here. She hasn't even gone to school yet. Why so early?" Then he thought of something, "And on what grounds?"

"We are acting on information received, Mr Armstrong."

Half laughing, Jay asked, "From whom, may I enquire?"

"I am not at liberty to divulge that, sir."

Eliza came through from the kitchen. She looked crumpled. Her eyes looked small and held no light. She was wearing the same clothes as yesterday. The previous two nights, in spite of Jay's exhortations and her own exhaustion, she had been unable to contemplate sleep. She had stayed up watching late night television in a mindless blank, taking none of it in until she finally slept for a few short hours on the three-seater. The feeling of sickness she'd had ever since learning of her mother's murder was still with her. She had eaten barely a thing since Monday and looked drained and haggard

"What's this about? Why so early?"

The policemen entered the house. Jay was white. His words explained exactly what this was about. "Surely you can't think we had anything to do with this? We loved and adored Annie – you cannot possibly believe otherwise. Whoever has told you otherwise is either deeply malicious or totally stupid. Whatever they said and whatever their reason, they are entirely wrong."

"I am sorry, sir," said the inspector," but as the closest relatives of Mrs Berkeley, you will appreciate that you are rather high on the list of potential suspects."

Eliza's legs felt unsteady, her face one of misery. "Are you suggesting either of us murdered my own mother? You must be mad!"

The policemen shuffled uneasily on their feet.

"Have the decency to allow me to explain to my daughters what you are doing here."

"Oh, yes, of course, Mrs Armstrong." The antagonism mustn't be allowed to build. The DI knew he had to keep Eliza on side as much as he was able. "Where are they now?"

"The youngest, Holly, is in the kitchen having breakfast. Can't you please at least wait until she goes to school? Juliet is still in bed."

"All right, Mrs Armstrong, we can wait until you have told Holly what's happening. When does she leave?"

"In about ten minutes."

"And how does she get there?"

"By bicycle to the station. She gets there on her own steam."

"Very well, we can hold off until then. But I must ask you both to remain where you are."

Holly appeared in the room. She scowled at the police then gaped in astonishment at the number of policemen standing about in their sitting room.

Eliza was so furious that she hadn't noticed her daughter come in behind her. "I'm supposed to be grateful for that, am I? This is just outrageous."

Holly, distressed said, "Why are they here, Mummy?"

"Don't worry, darling. The police are just doing their duty. We all need to know what happened to Annie B. and they're just going to hunt for any clues they might be able to find here." She hugged Holly. "It's all fine, really. I promise. Now, you should be off."

Eliza followed her to the door and waved as her daughter set off on her bike. In an effort to normalise the situation, trying to sound nonchalant and cheerful, she said what she always said, "Drive carefully."

She watched Holly pedal down the lane. Then she came back into the house, closed the door and returned to the sitting room. The detective nodded at the men who started to disperse around the house. One went into the kitchen and downstairs cloakroom, another hunted around the sitting room and playroom, and the two others went upstairs.

The detective stayed with Eliza and Jay and Juliet, who by this time had appeared. They sat, wretched and hardly speaking while the search took place.

After half an hour or so, one of the officers came into the room. "May I have a word, sir?" The senior investigating officer followed him to the kitchen doorway where the young officer whispered in his boss's ear.

The detective turned to Eliza and Jay. "Please remain where you are, I shall be back in a moment." The DI followed the officer through the kitchen and down the corridor that led to the downstairs cloakroom.

The cloakroom was a square tatty room that was used for hanging coats, macs, housing wellington boots and keeping fishing equipment, tools and other such things. At one end, a lavatory and basin were enclosed in a cubicle.

The two policemen reappeared in a few minutes, carrying Jay's toolbox, his Barbour jacket and what looked like a bagged pair of his gloves.

"Can you tell us whether these are your gloves, Mr Armstrong?" Jay agreed that they were, and the detective asked him again to verify what clothing he had been wearing on Monday morning. He told them and the officer returned to the cloakroom to collect Jay's flat cap and his Timberland boots.

His stammer back, he said, "I was going to suggest you take the pyjamas I wore in bed last night, and while we're at it, you might like my dressing gown." Starting to remove his dark blue towelling robe, Jay had one sleeve off and was almost beyond rage. "Actually, why not take all my clothes while you're at it?"

Eliza put a restraining hand on his arm. "Calm down, darling. You know they won't find anything, so calm down."

He exhaled noisily and issued a long groan. "I can't bear this, Eliza. They obviously think I did it."

"But we know you didn't, sweetheart, so they won't find anything."

"Mr Armsworth, we would ask you to accompany us to the police station to assist with our enquiries. You do not have to say anything. But it may harm your defence if you do not mention when questioned something that you later rely on in court. Anything you do say may be given in evidence. And now if you'd like to get dressed, the officer here will accompany you upstairs."

"My name is Armstrong! Jay Armstrong! May as well get that right if you're planning on charging me with the murder of a woman I adored and would never have harmed as long as I lived."

Eliza wondered if the policeman was trying to rile her poor husband by choosing one of his weak spots. She put her arms round Jay's neck and whispered, "Please calm down, darling. You need to keep calm. Do that deep breathing our yoga teacher taught us, remember?"

When Jay returned fully dressed, as he came into the room, one of the policemen was holding his laptop.

"Hey! That's my private laptop. You have no right–"

"This is a murder enquiry and I'm afraid we do, Mr Armstrong. Would you come with us, please?"

Eliza looked as though she might faint again. The shrill words sounded unnatural in her head. "When will he be back?"

"When Mr Armstrong has answered all our questions satisfactorily. This officer will remain here with you, Mrs Armstrong, and you are at liberty to invite anyone here, as long as you do not leave the house."

Eliza could not contain her sarcasm. "May as well lock us both up and throw away the–" She stopped mid-sentence. Suddenly she saw her mother in her head. The image she had was one of her smiling, with a finger to her lips.

"Okay," she said, calm again. She followed Jay as he got into one of the police cars, "I love you, darling. Everything is going to be all right. I know it."

He shouted back, "Ring Peter Fenton and tell him they're taking me to Cambridge!"

Eliza ran back into the house and immediately rang their solicitor as Jay had suggested. She cried and choked and shouted down the telephone.

Peter Fenton was only just able to understand what she was saying. He had of course read the papers and heard the news about Eliza's mother and was not altogether surprised to hear Jay was being questioned. *He would have,* Peter thought, *the most motive for her death.* Jay seemed a decent man, but Peter had dealt with enough people in his time to know that you should never judge a book by its cover.

"Please hurry, Peter."

"I'll need to send our top criminal lawyer, George Pearson. He's the best in Cambridge and a nice man. I'll go with him, Eliza. Try not to worry too much. The police often make mistakes. We're leaving right away."

He dropped everything he was doing and ran down the corridor of Fenton Barnard to George's office. They were round at the Parkside Police Station in no time. The Armstrongs were important clients.

Juliet was distraught and angry. Eliza rang Rose. "Can you come?" The cracked voice said it all.

"I'll be there straightaway, darling."

When she reached the farm, she found Eliza lying on the sitting room sofa in the foetal position, her legs bent up, her body curled round itself. Despair had overtaken her. Juliet, despite her intentions to be a rock to her mother, was lying on her bed crying her heart out.

22

7–8 NOVEMBER

At the pathologist's laboratory, an officer wearing blue latex gloves opened the toolbox. He carefully removed a large monkey wrench, which he had already bagged. With the pair of Jay's gloves and the clothes Jay had been wearing on the morning of the murder, he gave them to the forensic pathologist who had performed Annie's autopsy.

When she examined the wrench, there was a surprising amount of dried blood around the head of it that was clearly visible through the stereoscope. Some was visible to the human eye. If someone had tried to wash this tool, they had made a bad job of it. The pathologist suggested they might have been in a hurry.

A couple of broken white hairs were stuck in the clotted black blood that had seeped between the lower jaw and the screw mechanism of the tool. It also had a few tiny grey woollen fibres and some tiny yellow silk ones on the head and handle. The grey ones matched the gloves. The pattern on the injury was a telltale marker for the weapon that had inflicted it. A skin imprint in what remained of the scalp fitted with this. The pathologist had already taken photographic documentation of Annie's injuries and the pattern lacerations had wavelike characteristics imprinted from the teeth of the wrench.

Samples of the blood and the hair and their DNA were compared with that of the victim's. It was the same person. So, it was conclusive. This was the weapon that had killed the old lady.

The pathologist studied the wrench for fingerprints and found only Jay Armstrong's. She then looked closely at the woollen gloves that had rubber pads on the inside of the fingers. These had clearly not been washed and there were a few splatters of Annie's B.'s blood on the right glove. Again, the only fingerprints on them were those of Jay Armstrong's. Now the police had some positive evidence that pointed straight at the victim's son-in-law.

The pathologist carefully went over Jay's clothing to search for blood or any telltale signs that might indicate he had murdered the woman while wearing them. Here, she drew a blank. She phoned the DI who was at the police station interviewing Jay.

A young policeman knocked on the door of the interview room, put his head round the door and said, "Sorry to interrupt, governor, but I have something important for you to look at." The detective had left the room and returned a few minutes later with the wrench and the gloves. They had been bagged up again in clear plastic bags but were quite visible through them. He put them on the table.

"I understand the business you run with Mrs Armstrong has been in a spot of trouble lately?"

"It has been, yes, but things are much better now. We've had some good orders from the autumn catalogue."

"Have you been paid for those orders yet?"

"No. The money should come through very soon."

Jay did not know, but the police had secured a court order allowing them to access his personal and business bank accounts. They had seen that the business had been in trouble and that his personal funds were very low. They passed his laptop to an expert to hunt for any incriminating emails. The expert would also go through Jay's search history and see whether he really had been looking at the company website when he said he had. Search histories often revealed a lot about a suspect.

Delving into Anne Berkeley's background and her bank account, they could see that she had been a wealthy woman.

"Do you recognise this tool here, Mr Armstrong?"

Jay leant forward in his chair and studied the rusted old monkey wrench.

"Well, it looks like one I have, but mine hasn't been used for ages." He wanted to add "it's in my toolbox" but he had seen them removing it from his house and knew that that is where they had got the wrench.

The DI moved the wrench to one side, replacing it with the grey fishing gloves. "And the gloves? I believe you use them for fishing?"

Jay sighed. "They certainly look like mine."

"And when was the last time you wore them?"

"When I was fishing in Scotland in September."

"Have a close look at them, Jay." He could clearly see the spots of blood on the right hand one.

"What would you say about the blood on those gloves?"

"Must be from a fish. When I catch them, I gut them, you know."

"What if I told you the blood on that glove is actually human?"

"Maybe I nicked myself, I don't remember."

"That blood is Anne Berkeley's blood."

He went white. His jaw dropped.

"But how?"

"That's what I was hoping you could tell us, Jay."

The detective didn't need to reflect. It was a clear-cut case. They had a weapon, they had a pair of gloves and now they had the motive. A witness had come into the police station to say they had seen Jay Armstrong walking back across the field that morning carrying something about a foot long in one hand. The witness had insisted they be given anonymity so their evidence could not be used in the court trial, but it did help to decide the minds of the police. It had all happened so quickly since the search. That was on account of the witness. It had certainly been a helluva good tip-off, resulting in finding the perp a lot faster than they could have hoped. Now all that was needed was to inform the Crown Prosecution Service.

"Take him back to the cells, please." He'd let the man sweat a while longer.

The police rushed the weapon and gloves over to the CPS who had only to glance at the evidence to decide there was sufficient evidence to substantiate the charge of murder.

By about five o'clock that afternoon, Jay was brought back up from his cell to the custody sergeant, who handed him a charge sheet and read out the alleged offence to him. It was explained to him that he would be held at the station on remand until the date he was given to appear before the Cambridge Magistrate's court in two weeks' time. His case would then be passed on to the Crown Court for full trial with a judge and jury.

Jay was taken back down to his tiny, bare, windowless cell. He lay on the low narrow bed and turned toward the wall. He cried like he used to when a child.

The spectre of his stepfather that had haunted him for so many years had finally come to get him. His day of reckoning had arrived. He had deliberately let some of the air out of a tyre on Ralph's car, causing his death.

When Eliza rang the police to ask when they were going to return her husband to his home, they told her he had been charged with her mother's murder. She was unable to speak and dropped the landline phone so it smacked onto the kitchen floor. Its battery cover flew off. The batteries rolled across the terracotta tiles.

By Wednesday, still unable to eat and sapped of energy, Hugh Dunlop's exhausted body had tried to recuperate while he had lain in bed sleeping most of the day. His wife had rung the doctor, who had diagnosed a bad case of food poisoning, prescribed Dioralyte, plenty of water and no food. There was little he could do but wait it out.

On Thursday morning, having been assured the police had finished there, accompanied by the FLO, Eliza was determined to see where her mother had died. Frail as she was feeling, she managed to walk to the place where Annie had died.

When the officer had warned her that it would be a traumatic experience, she hadn't realised quite how bad it would be. They reached the place where the body had fallen. There were obvious signs of disturbance at the scene. Black, congealed blood covered some of the area. A cloud of blowflies rose into the air at the disturbance, some remaining along with their larvae.

Like Katie before her, Eliza threw up. Because of her mother's great love of nature and dislike of shop-bought flowers, she had hand-picked a bouquet of autumn berries and leaves and tied them with string. She quickly threw down the bunch to cover the disgusting sight and looked up at the sky.

Addressing the treetops, she said, "Wherever you are, I love you and want you to know that. I know about the cancer and wish you had shared it with me, but I understand why you didn't. You were so, so brave and I just wish I could say goodbye properly, and if you can hear me, I just want you to know we are so desperately sorry it had to end this way and we shall miss you terribly. You were the best mother I could have wished for, and Jay thinks so too. We all loved you so much. You know he didn't do this and so do I." She was barely able to finish, "I promise you, Mum, we will find whoever did this so you can sleep in the peace you deserve."

She dropped to her knees and wailed.

"There, you've told her, Mrs Armstrong. I'm sure your mum will be pleased to have heard from you and glad that you came. But it's time to come away now." The gentle officer helped her up and they walked home. It seemed to take forever.

That afternoon, Eliza took the first of the three one-hour visits a week that were allowed to Jay. For the second, she planned to take Juliet and Holly.

Still tearful, Jay walked slowly to the table between them. Crying also, she reached across for his hand. He did not take it. He looked grey.

She tried talking to him about what George Pearson was doing to help and she tried to bolster him. With no luck. In such a short time, her husband seemed to have almost lost touch with reality. All he would say was to keep insisting that this was his comeuppance and that justice had finally caught up with him.

Unable to make head or tail of what he was talking about, she finally said his name, "Jay! What are you trying to say?"

It was then, for the first time, he told her about what he had done to the tyre on Ralph's Ford Mustang. "I killed him, I killed him."

Her strength returned to her. She hissed at him, "You don't say a word of this to anyone else. Understand? You were abused, Jay, and you simply let the air out of a tyre. You didn't know he would die. And you didn't kill my mother!"

By Thursday morning, Hugh Dunlop had turned the corner. He got up and pottered about in his dressing gown. He was semi-retired and there was nothing especially pressing at the law firm. The office could wait. He would go in on Friday.

At supper, he managed to get down a couple of boiled eggs and toast, and afterwards he and his wife settled down on the sofa to watch a drama on television. Still feeling delicate, he stayed up to catch the news headlines but decided he would head back to bed after that.

Between the deep sonorous chimes of the Big Ben bell, the BBC newscaster read the headlines.

Bong, "Again, a mass shooting in the United States. This time twelve murdered in a Californian bar and dance hall."

Bong, "Suspect arrested for the murder of Mrs Anne Berkeley on Monday..."

Bong, "Mrs May talks of EU backstop to the backstop..."

"Oh my God! Oh no. It's true. Oh God!" Hugh Dunlop buried his head in his hands. His wife comforted him.

"Brexit is beyond our control, Hugh. What will be will be."

"I must go to the office."

"What? Now?"

"It's urgent."

The shock along with his recent poisoning was obviously making him confused. His wife said, in what she thought to be a calming tone, "I'm sure it'll wait till tomorrow."

"I can't believe I missed it. This is dreadful." Tears appeared in his eyes.

"Go back to bed, Hugh. You've had a horrible time and you're tired out."

"Early start," he muttered to himself as he left the room shaking his head, "early start. Important business. Oh dear, oh dear. Poor, poor Annie. This is so terribly sad. Oh dear, oh dear."

That night when Eliza had lain in bed, sleep had refused to come as questions had whirled around her troubled head. She was grieving on two accounts. But the business of Jay's arrest had not upset her as much as you might imagine. For a reason she would not have been able to explain, she was so certain of his innocence that she was convinced the Cambridge Police would soon realise their mistake too. She did not know about the evidence yet and might not have felt so optimistic if she had.

Staring at the ceiling, Eliza had gone over the many possibilities of who had actually done this frightful thing to her poor mum. Neither would she speak the words "murder" or "killing" or "death", nor even use them in her mind. She had not yet been able to process her mother's departure.

She thought about people from Heronsford. Why would any of them want to do such a thing? It was such a violent act, surely a woman couldn't do that to another? Or could they? But who? Rose? Eliza couldn't believe she was capable of such a terrible thing – unless, perhaps, she had known about Annie's cancer and it had been done to prevent her having to go through a dreadful, slow death. But then had she framed Jay for it. How, and why?

She racked her brains and recalled a recent heated exchange she and Jay had. This had been when he had yet again raised the issue that they should think about selling Manor Farm. She had become upset and now she remembered that Rose had been cleaning the kitchen and would have overheard what had turned into a furious argument. When she had asked Jay what might become of her mother if they were to sell, he'd shouted that her mother could stay in her barn for all he cared. Eliza had to remind him that under the terms of the original planning permission, the two properties could not be separated for sale. That had not helped Jay's mood.

Putting such dire thoughts out of her head, Eliza had decided her darling Rose could never murder Annie, even for the best possible reasons. So, who else could it be? Hamish? Bob? Stella? Patrick? Try as she might, there was absolutely no reason she could see why any of them would want to do away with such a well-loved old lady.

It must, she concluded, have been some random assailant who was up to no good in the wood and got caught out by Annie B. So, what were these things the police had taken from the house? Why Jay's tool-box? What had they got on him to arrest him?

She decided to call George Pearson in the morning. He would fill her in. Surely it couldn't have been Jay? Or could it? Had he been feigning love for Annie all these years? Getting rid of her mother would solve their financial problems as Eliza would inherit her money.

A tremor of fear ran through Eliza's body. She finally slept, the sleeping pill taking effect.

Finding Annie in the wood had a bad effect on Katie too. The whole experience had been traumatic for her. She had even been finger-printed by the police and questioned at length about exactly when she found Annie and whether she had rung them straightaway.

It almost felt as though they had doubted her word and however much Hamish had tried to reassure her that they were just doing their job, she had sunk fast into a deep depression, drinking more and more.

Her paranoia was increasing. Everything her husband did or said was suspicious to her. Something drastic had to be done. Hamish knew their lives had to change.

"I didn't want to tell you before, but since you are being so bloody stupid, it's time you heard the truth." Stella tried to interrupt but Bob's face stopped her. She went quiet.

"You may recall that your birthday is fast approaching. I had planned to give a surprise birthday party for you next month. As I couldn't mention it in front of you on Sunday, I dropped in at Manor Farm on Monday morning to give the Armstrongs their invitation. I rang the bell two or three times, but nobody came to the door. I gave up and as I was leaving, I saw Jay walking back across the field that leads from the farm to Rooks Wood. In one hand he was carrying something slim that was about a foot long. I thought nothing of it at the time and decided not to wait for him to return, and try again later. Jay is now being questioned. I didn't want to get my friend into trouble but after much deliberation, I decided that if Jay had really done something as appalling as murdering his elderly mother-in-law, then he deserved everything the police could throw at him."

"How could you?"

"Because my eyes did not deceive me. I know it's horrible to believe, but it looks like it's the truth."

"Jay loved Annie. I cannot believe he killed her."

"I don't want to think so either. I like Jay a lot. He's a good man. But I know what money problems can do to a person. Their company has hit the skids. He knows Annie's money will save the day."

"But they have been getting more orders recently and things are looking a bit better for them."

"Hmm... too little, too late?"

"I can't guess what the police have on Jay, but I suppose they must have some sort of evidence. Goodness knows what Eliza is thinking. I don't feel I can call her just yet. It's a terrible situation for her."

Was, they separately wondered, the dynamic between them beginning to alter?

23

9 NOVEMBER

On Friday morning, soon after nine o'clock, after the phone had rung for some time, an officer in charge of incoming calls at Parkside Police Station responded and said, "Cambridgeshire Constabulary. May I help you?"

"Oh, er, hello?" He gave his name. "I am a London solicitor requesting to speak to the detective in charge of the Anne Berkeley murder case."

"I'm afraid Detective Chief Inspector Waterman is out, sir."

"How can I get hold of him quickly? Does he have a mobile, please?"

"I'm sorry, sir, but we do not hand out officers' mobile phone numbers to members of the public."

"I am not a member of the public, I'm a solicitor."

"I see, sir," replied the sergeant patiently. "While I am sure you are telling the truth, unfortunately we do not hand out senior officers' mobile phone numbers. Do you wish to remain anonymous? In which case you need to–"

"No, I do not wish to remain anonymous. I wish to speak to Inspector Waterfield personally."

"Then I suggest you contact us after ten o'clock when Detective Chief Inspector *Waterman* will be present. You should be able to contact him via our live web chat service where you can explain what it is you want to tell him."

"Contact him through what, did you say?"

The sergeant sighed. Why did he have to deal with idiots all the time? "Our live web chat service. It's on our website," he said, still trying but failing to sound patient.

"Oh dear, however do I do that?"

Obviously old as the hills and thick as two planks. The sergeant took a deep breath. "Sir, the Inspector should be back by ten o'clock today. May I suggest you look up the website." Tempted to hang up on him, the frustrated policeman asked whether he had someone who could do it for him.

"Ah yes, an idea that. I'll ask my secretary to link me up to it. But I'd much rather speak to the detective."

"As I explained, I'm afraid he's a very busy man, sir."

"As I said, this is a highly important matter. I have information regarding the murder of Anne Berkeley."

Probably some crackpot calling, but you could never be sure. "Yes, sir. I am about to give you the department website address." The sergeant spelled out the address then slowly explained the process by which to engage with the live service. It took him some time since the man had first to find a pen as well as being seemingly computer illiterate. Once that was done, the sergeant said,

"Ask your secretary to put you on to the chat service." The solicitor muttered under his breath, wondering what the world had come to. He thanked the officer, who he felt had actually been pretty unhelpful and the two men gratefully rang off.

Soon after this, Eliza received a call from the solicitor.

Having had a very late night at the station, Inspector Waterman was expecting today to be the same. The Anne Berkeley case had been dealt with but there was always too much to be done. A hearty breakfast before work helped him get through. He ate at a nearby café and by 9.50, was back at his desk.

"Er, excuse me, sir." The sergeant who had spoken to the solicitor told him about the call.

"What's he got to say about the murder, I wonder?"

"Could be a hoax, sir, but you never know. I directed the man to speak on the live web chat service. I'll find out whether he has called yet."

He hurried off, returning soon with information that the operator had spoken to the man, verified who he was with a quick check, returned the man's call and passed the DCI's email address on to him. Dunlop was the name.

The detective tapped his email open and there it was. He read through the email and its three attachments. He moved quickly and called the officer back in, "Get these printed for me straightaway, please, and bring them back immediately."

When he had finished re-reading it, he dropped the paper on his desktop, sighed, rubbed his greying temples and leant back in his chair. In all his years, he had never come across anything like this.

The email was from the solicitor who had called him earlier. It had two attachments and was marked urgent. The first attachment was a sworn statement, the second Hugh Dunlop's affidavit. He read through them.

He had got the wrong man in the cells. At least, it looked that way. But that man's fingerprints and Anne Berkeley's blood were on the monkey wrench and his gloves, and no-one else's.

The first thing to do was re-examine the evidence. He buzzed the internal phone through to ask for the file to be brought to him at once.

Just after 2.30 on Friday afternoon, Alan Waterman and three other officers visited Heronsford Manor. The door was opened by the housekeeper. She explained that Mr McKenzie was at work in Cambridge, but that Mrs McKenzie was in her sitting room. Would they like to speak with her? They stepped into the big hall that lead to various downstairs rooms in the house, along with a grand curling staircase with a shining mahogany bannister rail that, wider at the bottom, narrowed as it ascended to a small central landing where it split into two parts that led upstairs.

The anxious-faced housekeeper fetched Stella, who looked taken aback by the police presence. This was the second time they had called that week. They had seen the couple early on Tuesday before Bob had gone to work and the shocked pair had little to tell.

Assuring her she had nothing to be alarmed about, the inspector showed Stella a warrant he had to search the house. As though she didn't trust her legs to hold her up, she sat down on a chair in the hall.

"Why? What for?"

Stella asked the housekeeper, who was quietly listening behind the kitchen door, to accompany the men around the house. Waterman stayed with Stella, assuring her that they were simply following up on some information received. But, she asked, what was it to do with? Was she or Bob in trouble? If so, for doing what? Did this have to do with Annie Berkeley's murder? The inspector avoided replying and simply suggested she didn't worry too much at this stage of their enquiry.

The police asked the housekeeper what day the bins were collected, to which she replied, "Early on Monday mornings."

"And what about the laundry?"

The housekeeper took a moment to think about her routine. "Well, each day I take dirty laundry from Mr and Mrs McKenzie's separate laundry baskets and bring it downstairs. But the washing is done twice a week."

Inspector Waterman narrowed his eyes. "What about silk handkerchiefs, for instance? Washed or dry cleaned?"

"They are always handwashed and ironed with care here, sir," said the housekeeper proudly.

"Thank you."

The two officers who had been assigned to search through the rubbish bins were under instructions to sift through them with great attention. They soon reappeared with something packaged.

Stella tried but could not see what it was. They had been briefed beforehand on what to do with their find. One of them said something quietly in the detective's ear. He nodded and watched them leave the house. They drove away fast.

Meantime, the housekeeper showed two others to Robert and Stella's bedroom suite that consisted of a large bedroom, a dressing room for Bob and another for Stella. They also had separate bathrooms. The policeman quietly whistled.

He searched through Bob's built-in wooden floor-to-ceiling wardrobe that covered the entire length of his dressing room. One end contained rows of shoes carefully placed on racks that pulled out, above which hung ties, belts and scarves. Next to that were sliding drawers that held carefully pressed folded shirts and jumpers. The centre two hanging rails held jackets, waistcoats and trousers while at the end, stacks of shallow drawers that slid open contained socks, boxer shorts, cufflinks, watches and handkerchiefs. The officer checked through the wardrobe as well as the laundry baskets that were both empty.

He then checked Stella's dressing room and searched through her things that were kept in a similar arrangement to her husband's. He combed the bedroom and the bathrooms. When he had finished, he descended the staircase holding a large evidence bag.

"I'm done, boss."

"Right. You know what to do, Daniels." The officer nodded, left the house, got into the inspector's car.

Before he left to join him, the inspector suggested strongly to both Stella and the housekeeper that they kept quiet about their visit, in particular to Mr McKenzie, and assured them both not to worry. Waterman and Daniels drove quickly away.

24

9–18 NOVEMBER

O nce the two police cars had left Heronsford Manor, Alan Waterman placed his siren on the roof of what was his own car – the cutbacks had dire effects on the force – and sped back to Cambridge. However fast he wanted to get to the pathologist's laboratory, the rush hour traffic held him up.

At least, he thought, *the officer who left earlier should have got there before the build-up of cars mostly full of children from private schools heading home from four o'clock onwards.* That was the first evidence he wanted forensics to look at but the second that he had with him now was also vital.

There was no DNA on the wrench as the perp had been careful enough to pick it up with something. The pathologist re-inspected and found fibres from the yellow silk handkerchief taken from Bob's drawer on the monkey wrench. Recent research had proved that thinner gloves, mostly latex ones, would still leave a fingerprint through the glove. When the forensic pathologist was asked to re-examine the fishing gloves, he turned the gloves inside out and found fingerprints had transferred through the latex. Alan Waterman sighed with relief and gratitude to modern forensic science for the continued breakthroughs they made when it came to catching criminals.

Late on Friday evening, the front doorbell at Heronsford Manor rang again. The housekeeper was off duty now, so it was answered by Bob.

"Good Lord above, what are you lot doing here at this hour?" A thunderous expression on his face, he said, "What d'you want now? It's bloody late and–"

They stepped into the hall. Waterman said, "Robert McKenzie, you are under arrest on suspicion of the murder of Anne Berkeley. You do not have to say anything, but it may harm your defence if you do not mention when questioned something which you later rely on in court. Anything you..." The last bit of the short speech was drowned by Bob.

"How bloody dare you? D'you know who I am? This is a fucking travesty! Stella! Stella! Where the hell is the woman? You've already had my witness statement, you bloody idiots. Jay Armstrong did it. I saw the man coming back across the field, for God's sake! Why would I kill an old woman? You're bloody mad. I've given you your man, already." He bellowed again, "Stella! Stella! Come here at once!"

She came running through the hall. "Whatever is happening?"

"They're arresting me for Annie's murder. It's just bloody ridiculous! Tell them I was here with you that morning."

Stella was trembling. "He was here with me."

"Call my solicitor, immediately!" Whatever he said, however much he protested, they cuffed him and took him back to Parkside.

In the police station interview room, they sat Bob down to wait for his solicitor to arrive. Inspector Waterman saw a new side to the man who had now calmed down, had apologised for yelling and was being what the detective would describe as a cross between smarmy and something else that he could not quite name. When McKenzie's bemused solicitor arrived, they commenced the interview.

They placed six items in clear plastic bags marked "evidence" on the desk. One was a bright yellow silk handkerchief. They asked Bob if it was his.

"I have one very like it."

"I suggest this is your handkerchief, Mr McKenzie, as it has your DNA on it."

"Okay, then it's mine. So?"

Waterman pointed to the tweed jacket with the red satin lining. "And is this your jacket, Mr McKenzie?"

"Probably. Certainly like one I have."

Waterman pushed forward Jay's fishing gloves. "Ever seen these before?"

"Not to my knowledge. They look like fishing gloves. Not mine."

He pointed to the monkey wrench. "And this object?"

"What are you trying to get at? I've never seen that before. Don't even know what it is. I generally pay workmen who use that sort of thing to do things for me."

"And these?" He moved the fifth item in front of Bob. It was a pair of latex gloves.

Bob shook his head in amazement. "What the hell is this?"

"Answer the question please, Mr McKenzie."

"Never seen them before."

"And, finally, this?" It was a box of "Handy Latex Disposable Gloves".

Bob threw his hands in the air, glanced at his solicitor and shrugged his shoulders. "I honestly don't know what you are talking about. I've never seen that box before."

Waterman pointed at the fishing gloves.

"With regard to this pair of, as you rightly call them, fishing gloves, they bear traces of Anne Berkeley's blood." He moved the wrench in front of Bob. "As does this wrench that was used to kill her."

Bob sighed. "Look, I was very upset to learn of Annie B.'s murder and as I told you before, on Monday morning I saw Jay Armstrong walking back across the field from the wood where she was found. He was carrying something that could very well have been that thing." He gestured toward the wrench. "You've got your man. Why are you doing this to me?"

"Because, Mr McKenzie, that handkerchief left some fibres on the wrench. We know you were wearing it in your jacket front pocket on Sunday. And those gloves come from this packet here that was found in the laundry room of your house."

"How would I know a thing like that? The housekeeper deals with cleaning and that sort of thing. I told you I've never seen that box or those gloves before."

"Then can you explain how your DNA got on them and how they bear traces of red satin fibres that exactly match the lining of your jacket pocket? And how come your fingerprints, along with traces of latex, have been found inside the fishing gloves?"

Bob went quiet. He shrugged and looked at DCI Waterman, who now was able to describe the attitude he had glimpsed earlier. *Smug was the word; smug.*

The solicitor whispered to his client.

DCI Waterman continued, "I put it to you that you did murder Anne Berkeley with that wrench, wearing those fishing gloves over that pair of latex gloves. I put it to you that you took the wrench and the fishing gloves from the Armstrong family cloakroom when they were entertaining you for lunch. I believe that in order to prevent your fingerprints or DNA being transferred, you used your handkerchief to pick these items up and that you wrapped the weapon in the handkerchief and hid the gloves in your jacket pocket. I suggest you did this in order to implicate Jay Armstrong in the murder."

"Ridiculous! You are complete idiots!"

The solicitor leant sideways to murmur in his ear again.

Then Bob added, "No comment." He said this with an arrogant smile or, more accurately, a smirk.

The total, sheer arrogance of the man. Waterman had already decided to keep the real bombshell for the trial.

At this time, Eliza received a three-page letter written in fountain pen on blue Basildon Bond writing paper. It had a London postmark and it arrived on a Saturday. It was just after the police had delivered Jay home with many apologies for the wrongful arrest.

Manor Farm Barn

Sunday 4 November 2018

My very darling Eliza,

I have given this to Hugh Dunlop to post to you. Hugh will have contacted you and you will by now have read a copy of the statement I have sent to the Cambridgeshire Constabulary. During the coming week, I expect to meet my death at the hands of Bob McKenzie. Of course, there is the possibility that I am wrong about him and if I am, you will never receive this. But I think I am right and wonder what Mr M. will cook up for me.

I felt very sad earlier but now I am fine and not afraid. The thing that makes me most sorrowful is not to be able to say goodbye to you properly. To hug and hold you and tell you how very much I have always loved you. To tell you how I wish I didn't have to leave you and how that is the biggest wrench for me now. I hope this letter will manage to express how deeply I feel about you.

If you were ever in doubt, I loved your father as much. I wasn't the wife I set out to be and failed him in a number of ways. He failed me in others. By and large, we were very happy together and perhaps surprisingly, our later years turned out to be some of our happiest times. When he died, I missed him deeply. I know you did too.

A decoy in a game of chess is a strategy that lures an enemy piece to an unfavourable position. A decoy hopefully tricks your opponent into deflecting a piece to a square you

██████████████████

want them to move to. If it works, it creates a diversion so
you can take control of a situation. In my end game, it was
Bob's turn to move. He had to move or lose altogether so his
only option was to do away with me. Of course, he did not
know it was a decoy. Remember, I think he has already
killed two people and he has to be stopped.

I know you will be very angry with me for excluding you
from news of my health. I had planned to tell you about the
cancer but was putting it off as long as possible to spare us
both. I didn't dare tell you about this plan for fear you'd try
to stop me. I just hope that in time you will forgive and
understand the reasoning behind what I did.

Darling, I have been dreading months of agony ahead
before dying a painful, miserable death. I am not brave
enough to take my own life and nor did I think that would
be fair on you. When the chance came to catch an evil
murderer and to end my own life a little prematurely but
less painfully, it seemed the perfect opportunity to make my
departure. Far from brave, I suppose you could say I am a
coward to have chosen this path. If I have played my
endgame well, I know Mr McKenzie will do the job quickly
and properly. No chancer that one, he is a methodical,
clever killer who is likely to try to make my killing look like
an accident. Whatever the police do, be sure to pressure them
to search thoroughly for evidence, in particular with regard
to DNA. He knows what he is doing and will try everything to
cover his tracks. If you read this before he is caught, please

2

██████████████████

show it to them and, if necessary, beg them to re-examine evidence.

I don't need to ask, for I know you will look after my little Mildred for me. She hasn't long left herself, so would you be extra-loving to her during that time? She is much too practical and self-centred to miss me for more than a day or so and will simply move in with you without batting an eye. Don't forget, she has always slept on my bed!

If you need me, in a sense I shall still be around, so talk to me. But somehow, my lovely girl, I don't think you will miss me for long. You are wise, strong and lead your life well. You have demonstrated that you are someone who does not give up in the face of difficult times. I love you, Jay and my grandchildren very much indeed. Please tell them the truth and try to explain that I did what I did for what I believed was the good of everyone, them included.

Yours always,

Mum xx

Her mother had been mistaken in assuming Bob would make her death look like an accident but had been right about how he would come up with some way to try to protect himself from being caught. That he had planned to incriminate Jay in his diabolical scheme had again demonstrated what a conscience-free monster he was.

Having Jay home was such a relief. The man she adored had returned from being AWOL and was hers once again. His experience in prison had altered him. For the better. He had developed a new attitude towards what he had always thought of as success. He realised now that success was about making the best of life and what you have. Not about getting more.

He felt stronger and now able to cope with whatever life threw at him. Unburdening himself of the terrible secret that had dogged him all those years had been a cleansing experience.

He'd had time in custody to think about his role in the death of his appalling stepfather and had exonerated his boy self from blame. After all, as Eliza had said, he had just let the air out of a car tyre.

Trying to discover whether her mother had known how seriously ill she actually was, Eliza visited Dr Gordon. He explained that she most certainly knew.

"A battle-axe to the very end," she said.

"And a very fine and particularly brave battle-axe she was."

"What I still can't quite believe is that if the cancer was so far advanced, how she could still have been walking and why wasn't she bed-bound?"

"It is possible for a person with stage four pancreatic cancer to walk unaided. This cancer can lead to a person losing muscle strength and overall fitness. A few individuals maintain physical fitness even while having cancer. Your mother was one of them. A great advertisement for keeping active as she did. I imagine she was in a lot of pain but did her best to disguise it. She really was remarkable." He hung his head and when he looked up again, Eliza saw his eyes were glazed.

"She was," said Eliza. She leant forward and reached for his hand. He gave it to her. "We've known one another since I was born. My mother was terribly fond of you and as a family we are so grateful for everything you have done for us, often way beyond the call of duty. Thank you from us all."

"I can honestly say it really was my pleasure. I shall miss your mum very much."

25

MID-NOVEMBER TO MID-DECEMBER

Searching for correspondence from the hospital, Eliza lowered the hinged fall front of her mum's old oak antique bureau. At the back of the desk was an arrangement of cubbyholes for stationery and document drawers with tiny brass knobs. It was usually stacked high with letters and documents, but Annie had evidently had a clear out.

Eliza found nothing of any help and she was about to close the front when she noticed a lower right-hand drawer slightly open. She suddenly remembered its secret. As a little girl, one day she had arrived in the sitting room to find her mother sitting at the desk when the drawer had been removed from its casing. At the bottom a hidden slide compartment was open.

Quickly closing it, her mother had quietly said, "This is Mummy's secret drawer. Our special secret, okay? And we won't tell anyone about it, will we? And it's just for Mummy, no-one else, not even Eliza, so Eliza won't ever look in it, will she? Promise?" Vehemently, shaking her head from side to side, Eliza had promised and then Rose had appeared, taken her hand and whisked her off to do something or other.

For all those years, Eliza had stuck to her promise. In what now felt like a betrayal, she removed the drawer and opened the compartment below, where on top of letters and appointments from Addenbrookes Hospital, she found an old brown envelope inside a blue one marked "Eliza" in ink.

Having read through the statement that would be used in court, the severe ache of distress that had enveloped Eliza then would not leave her. Now it almost overwhelmed her. Her mother had done all this without allowing her only close relative to accompany and lend her support. As her mother had known it would, this made Eliza feel so indignant. Ever since discovering the truth, the question had been whirling around her brain. Why hadn't she trusted her daughter to share this burden?

Breathing hard, she sat down on the old Chippendale-style chair in front of the desk. The indefinable feeling that raced round her now might have been anger, but somewhere inside she knew it was really the bizarre sense that however shocking her mother's death had been, it had saved them from a great deal worse. But that was her mum all over, independent and determined.

Eliza hunched over in the chair and rocked her body as she howled tears that were a blend of grief and guilt. If she had done something sooner, paid more attention to her mother's state of health, been more watchful, more hands-on... But then she realised that the other terrible events in Heronsford had absorbed her time and that her mum's own stubbornness had delayed taking herself to the doctor.

Her mother had known this would happen. She had cleared the rest of her desk. The only things she had kept were the hospital correspondence and appointments and the letter for her daughter from a deep understanding that humans are even more curious than monkeys. *At least*, she thought, *her mother would have relished some enjoyment from leaving the drawer pulled forward as a clue.*

She opened the brown envelope. Addressed to Anne Berkeley at Manor Farm, the postmark read London SW1 27 Oct, 1987 5.30pm. It had evidently once been opened with a paper knife and looked as though it had contained an invoice. Eliza pulled it out to find it was in fact a handwritten note on the torn-out page of a notebook. There was no address at the top.

26th October

My beloved Annie,

I have read, re-read and read again your letter. My heart feels broken, all the more for knowing that you too are hurting and that your goodness impelled you to write it. You are inescapably right and had I not found so unbearable the thought of being without you, I might have written a similar message to you. The small hope I have left for us both is that by saving our marriages, we may in years come to find satisfaction from having done what we did. I know the pain I feel will continue for a long time and that I shall carry on loving and being proud of you.

Remain strong and brave, my darling. I kiss you,

Michael x

Written a little over thirty years ago the sad little note was a simple reminder. Her mother had been young once and privy to dreams and sexual desires like everyone else. Eliza sat for a while longer on the chair with its faded green velvet seat in front of the old bureau, the letter on her lap. She wondered who Michael had been. From the way his letter was worded, he sounded sophisticated and Eliza guessed the most likely person would have been someone in the same profession as her mum. Perhaps, he had also been a barrister or even a judge.

But why had she decided to let Eliza in on this secret from the grave? Eliza guessed the sharp old girl had somehow figured out about the short-lived affair Eliza had with Hamish. This had lasted a few months when things had been so difficult with Jay and tragedies were occurring like volcanic eruptions. Each had always admired and liked the other and they had felt some closeness that became a means of consolation for their unhappiness. They had both soon made themselves draw a line under it with some relief and were now glad they had done so.

Eliza realised that her mum had left this very personal memento of a time in her life that had been difficult in the spirit of understanding that things had not been easy for Eliza. In a sense, it gave her the okay for having contemplated another life with another man. But that had not been the true point, Eliza was sure. Her mum was simply demonstrating her own frailty in these matters and letting her daughter know that she didn't need to feel her mother had been so hard to live up to. *That canny old bird,* thought Eliza, *there had been little that had escaped her notice or her thinking.*

A couple of weeks later, Eliza received a phone call from Stella. She asked whether they could meet up somewhere quiet where they could talk. A suspicion niggling at her that Stella would try to convince her that Bob was not guilty, Eliza was unsure whether she was doing the right thing when she agreed to do so. So that no prying Heronsford eyes or ears could see or hear, they agreed to meet in Cambridge two days later.

At 11.30am in the Café Noir on Bridge Street near the River Cam, Eliza sat waiting. Sitting at a table beside the window, she had no interest in the sluggish, dirty river drifting past or the few desultory ducks hanging about near the edge in hope of some titbits. Today was too cold for anyone to think of feeding them.

She wondered why she had bothered to come too. Since her mother's killing, she had felt disconnected from life and the events that continued around her. She was what people call 'managing', but the friends who told her how well she was doing could not see beneath the surface she presented. Inside she was struggling, misery threatening to consume her. Colour gone from her life, she felt tired and empty all the time, as though she were a hologram of herself simply going through the motions of being who she was.

Recognising that she was close to a proper breakdown, the previous week she had taken herself to see Dr Gordon who had prescribed a course of antidepressants that he assured her would start to kick in soon. She was still waiting for something happen that could make her feel better. Things with Jay had improved a lot, the company was back in business but still she felt divorced from it all.

Avoiding Eliza's eye as much as she could, Stella arrived and approached her table. Giving her a brief peck on the cheek, she took off her coat, draped it over the back of her chair and sat down opposite Eliza. She had decided beforehand that she would start straightaway with what she wanted to say. She knew Eliza would have no wish for small talk or niceties and she was spot on.

She ordered a coffee but didn't wait for its arrival before she first told how wonderful she had thought Annie B. was and told her about that day in late October when she bumped into her mother on the London train. She explained that they had got talking about her marriage to Bob. There was something about the way Annie B. listened with such care and perspicacity that she had felt she could see beneath her pretence that all was well. Perhaps it had been because Stella's own mother was so far away or because Annie B. had such a wise, maternal way about her, that had made her burst into tears and pour out her heart to her.

Stella told Eliza what she had revealed to Annie B. While she was telling her, she couldn't prevent herself from sobbing. She recounted how abusive Bob had been towards her, mostly mentally but on a couple of occasions physically, once when he had smacked her face and another when he had kicked her leg. There was, she had explained to Annie B., something innately angry and violent in the man that he generally kept well hidden, but that she had witnessed enough to scare her. When she had threatened to leave him, he had given her the cold warning that he would kill her without hesitation. Stella said he had bragged about having an affair with Louise. It had surprised Stella that Annie told her that she had already harboured strong suspicions that Bob had psychopathic tendencies.

Stella had the feeling that somehow her revelations on the train were in some way connected with it. On the Saturday afternoon, she continued, the day before they had lunched at Manor Farm, the housekeeper had told her that Annie B. had delivered a letter for Bob. Stella had not mentioned it to him as he was "funny" about what he considered his personal affairs and would be annoyed if she had. That is how frightened she was of her husband, who, she added, she had come to hate with a deep loathing. She had waited for him to tell her what it was about. But he had not said a word about it, which had made her feel very uncomfortable. Whatever had Annie B. written to him that was so urgent it couldn't have been sent in the post? She had prayed it had not been to do with the conversation they'd had on the train but had a nasty feeling it may have been. Since the police had charged him, she had searched through the house to find the letter. Being Bob, he had made sure to destroy it.

Eliza had sat quietly listening to all this in amazement. And relief. She had assumed Stella would be upset about Bob's arrest and this had been the last thing she had been expecting. In a small way, it made her feel a little better. It felt as though the two of them were women who had suffered in very different ways but on account of the same man.

When Stella finished what she had to say, while the shaking woman was blowing her nose and wiping her eyes, Eliza leant forward, stretched her arms across the table and took Stella's hands in hers.

"I was just learning to love your mother very much, and now she is gone."

The women squeezed each other's hands. Together they bawled their hearts out.

The same morning that Stella was meeting Eliza in Cambridge, Patrick was doing a last-minute check around Sparepenny Place where everything was packed ready for the removal company the following morning. He searched through cupboards making sure they were empty.

When he got to Sinead's old room, he got onto his hands and knees to open a small cupboard on the floor. Right at the back he found a dusty shoebox. In it were Eliza's engagement ring, Jay's credit card, Johnny's iPhone and a dried-up flower head that he didn't know was from Rose's garden. He took the box downstairs and was just placing it on his hall table when a sudden anxiety shot through him. He had remembered something. He crossed to the inglenook chimney and reached up inside to produce a soot-covered, white crumpled handkerchief. He took this into the garden and burnt it. The blackened fragments were caught by the wind and blown across the now covered swimming pool.

He remembered the day when, having checked Louise was working in her dark room, he had taken a taxi and told the driver to wait on the back road. He had told the driver he was arranging a surprise for his wife. That had been completely true.

Then, having taken the padlock key for the back gate earlier, he had run through the trees into the garden. He recalled slipping off his T-shirt and shorts, dashing into the dark room, surprising Louise, putting his arms round her waist.

He remembered his own fear as he had stuffed the hanky into her mouth and half carried, half dragged the terrified woman to the poolside. There, with her in his grip, he had jumped into the pool and held her under the water. It hadn't taken long. He'd had so little time. But all he had needed to do was to put his body across hers and hold her under. Once she was dead, leaving her in the pool, he had rapidly dried with the towel he had brought with him and thrown his clothes on again. Then he had legged it through the front gateway, turned left out of the drive and around the corner to the back road to the waiting taxi. No-one could have seen him. It had been as pre-meditated as it gets.

He had just had as much as a man can take. Louise had waved her affair in Patrick's face and threatened to run off with Bob. Perhaps she had been hoping to provoke him into leaving her. If so, she had underestimated his love for his daughter.

While the furniture van was loading up, he returned the stolen things to their owners. They all sympathised deeply with the state poor Sinead had been in and agreed never to mention it again. If it wasn't for his darling Cambridge girlfriend, he knew he wouldn't have been able to live with what he had done. Guilt acquired even in innocence or error can hound a person as long as they live, let alone if it is a real guilt. He prayed that in time it would subside and that his girlfriend would become his wife and a stepmother for Sinead.

For the meantime, Sinead was loving Francesca's cat Thai who now slept on her bed in their new house.

Hamish and Katie were sitting quietly on the bench in their garden, gazing at the fields and woods beyond. Hamish had done the thing he had been planning to do the day of Annie B.'s murder. He had handed in his notice and left the following day.

Hamish said quietly, "You know, our marriage and our happiness are far more important than anything else. If we are happier, our kids will be too. I love you, Katie Nicholson, and I think you love me. All we need to do to make it work is to join forces and set up our own business. 'Wood Farm Products.' I make the drinks and you the sauces and ice creams. How's about it, old girl?"

Suddenly, in a sentence, Katie's life changed. It was an amazing experience and, in that moment, all her insecurities began to melt away. Her man loved her. He wanted to be at home with her full-time. He wanted to work alongside her and she knew then and there that they could make this work. She had not felt so good or so clear-headed for years. She jumped up and ran around in little circles shouting to the sky,

"Eat and drink your way back to happiness with Wood Farm Products!"

Then she threw her arms around Hamish's neck and smothered him with kisses. He stood up and lifted his wife up high off the ground. She wrapped her legs around his waist while he danced across the garden. The birds in the trees, the ducks on the pond, the chickens in their enclosure, the sheep in the field, all stopped for a moment to wonder whether they should flee from the fearful sound of the raucous laughter that filled the air.

26

FEBRUARY, THE FOLLOWING YEAR

None of them went to the trial except Stella and Rose. Consumed with rage as they both were, they wanted to see the bastard get his desserts. Annie B.'s statement was read out by the prosecution.

To the Senior Investigating Officer in charge of the investigation into the murder of Anne Berkeley

Affidavit of Anne Berkeley QC

Name: *Anne Berkeley, QC Criminal Defence Barrister (retired)*

Address: *Manor Farm Barn, Heronsford, Cambridge CB22 4HZ*

Date of Birth: *14 March 1944*

I, Anne Berkeley, state on oath that the following facts in this statement are entirely true and that they come from my personal knowledge. I am writing this in the presence of my solicitor, Mr Hugh Dunlop, whose sworn affidavit is also enclosed with this statement. I have asked Mr Dunlop to ensure that in the event of my death during the next seven days by unnatural cause or unusual means, perhaps even appearing accidental, that this affidavit is passed on as soon as possible to the Cambridgeshire Constabulary.

On Tuesday, 30 October 2018, I took the 11.06am train from Heronsford Station to London Liverpool Street. At the station, I met Mrs Stella McKenzie of The Manor, Heronsford, Cambridge. She was also on her way to London. During the journey, Stella McKenzie and I sat opposite from one another on the train with no-one else sharing our double seats, which were either side of a table. We had a long conversation in which a tearful Mrs McKenzie informed me that her husband, Robert McKenzie, was mentally abusive to her in private, calling her names, intimidating and making threats to her, shouting at her, acting aggressively toward her, undermining her and telling her what she could and couldn't do. The abuse included refusing to allow her to work as a model, as she had done before marrying him.

Stella McKenzie also told me that Robert McKenzie bragged to her that he'd had an affair with Mrs Louise Ryan of Sparepenny Place, Heronsford, who died by drowning in her swimming pool in June this year. Although the verdict of her unusual death was death by misadventure, my personal belief is that Robert McKenzie was her murderer. How he did it, leaving no trace of his DNA or any other evidence, I have no idea.

When Mrs McKenzie had asked for a divorce and attempted to leave her husband, he told her that he would kill her if she tried and has made a number of threats on her life. She has been living in extreme fear of her husband.

I saw the couple together a number of times and could see that while Robert McKenzie was clearly entranced by and proud of his wife, it was plain that he controlled her.

On Saturday, 28 July, the annual Heronsford Fête was held at Heronsford Manor, home of Robert and Stella McKenzie. I saw Robert McKenzie carrying Stella's chihuahua dog across the garden and disappear into what is called the Contemplative Garden, an area hidden by tall yew hedges from the rest of the garden. Later, the dog's corpse was found in one of the ponds, thereby implicating one

Manor Farm Barn, Heronsford, Cambridge CB22 4HZ

of the many people attending the fête. I believe Robert McKenzie killed the animal as when I saw him ten minutes later, he did not have the dog with him.

On Saturday, 4 August, soon after 11.00pm, following a late supper with my friend Mrs Pam Sowerby of Hope House, Church Road, Heronsford, I drove home past Smith's Cottage where Ms Francesca Bianchi lived. That was the night her cottage caught on fire and she died inside. I saw Robert McKenzie on the cottage doorstep being welcomed by Ms Bianchi. I believe him to have deliberately set fire to the cottage because Ms Bianchi had gossiped that Louise Ryan was having an affair. I know this because my daughter told me Ms Bianchi had mentioned it at a lunchtime barbecue that same day. This was a day the wives had congregated since the men had been away fishing for the day. The coincidence that I saw Robert McKenzie at Ms Bianchi's house late that evening, seems too great to be dismissed. I would guess that his wife must have told him about Ms Bianchi's gossip.

I am suffering from advanced pancreatic cancer. My GP is Dr Edward Gordon, The Surgery, Heronsford, Cambridge CB22 4RG, and he will confirm this. Having chosen to forego chemotherapy that might prolong my life by a few months, I have been told I can expect between two and four months left to live. I am aware that these remaining months will involve a highly debilitating and painful lead up to a very unpleasant death.

Manor Farm Barn, Heronsford, Cambridge CB22 4HZ

Having heard Stella McKenzie's story and having reached my own judgement, I made the choice that I would use my death as a lure in an attempt to entrap what I am convinced is an astute and calculating murderer. By means of offering Robert McKenzie forty-eight hours to hand himself over to the police with a full confession to the murders of Louise Ryan and Francesca Bianchi, I intended to provoke him into committing murder upon myself. I wrote a letter to Robert McKenzie telling him what I thought but not what I had heard from his wife, for fear she would bear recrimination from her husband.

> I have had many dealings with Cambridgeshire Constabulary over the years and I consider it to be a very fine police force indeed. I sincerely believe your men will make every effort and succeed in catching and charging Robert McKenzie with murder.

Manor Farm Barn, Heronsford, Cambridge CB22 4HZ

Although Annie's identification of Bob seen entering Smith's Cottage on the night of the fire held some weight, there was no actual proof that he had deliberately set the fire, so reluctantly the police had to agree they could not indict him for that murder. As a result of no evidence, the police couldn't prosecute him, but the prosecution made sure the jury knew about Louise's death and her affair with McKenzie and his probable role in Francesca's murder.

The jury took no time to reach a unanimous decision that the defendant was guilty of Anne Berkeley's murder. In Judge Golding's summing up, he called McKenzie "an evil, manipulative and dangerous man who must never be allowed consideration of parole". Robert McKenzie was given a full life sentence that, in the judge's words meant "the full twenty-five years". He was sent to Whitfield Prison in Norfolk.

EPILOGUE

I hover, I vibrate and I watch. I don't feel cold or hot or pain or any external feelings.

He called "Eliza" and "Jay" softly. When he got no response, he went as quietly and quickly as he could to the downstairs cloakroom. I saw him remove a pair of latex gloves from his pocket and put them on. From a carrier bag he took out a strange-looking pair of woollen gloves with rubber pads on the palms.

Then he pulled out a large monkey wrench. So that was what he killed me with. No wonder it hurt. He put it back where I suppose it ordinarily lived in Jay's toolbox. Then, in one of the old oak cubbyholes in which we had always kept such things, he replaced what I now realised were Jay's fishing gloves. He must have grabbed the wrench and gloves when he went to the loo after lunch on Sunday. What a quick-thinking bastard he is.

When he washed his hands, which he did very thoroughly, I know he felt the full power of my hatred. He glanced at himself in the wall mirror and a shudder of extreme anxiety coursed through him. Not something the man is used to, angst being foreign to him. Then he sneaked back through the house and was gone before being noticed by either Jay or Eliza. He must have had a prepared excuse for calling round but had no need to use it.

I stayed as close as I could to Eliza while she was in the bath. I know she felt my presence and thought about me, but I wasn't able to influence her to get out of it and catch the man red-handed – literally – with my blood on his hands, or at least poor Jay's gloves. I was desperate to let her know but there was no way I was able. I just had to hover and watch and hone in. I was always concerned that my statement might not have been enough to find him guilty, but it did get them to re-examine the case and release poor Jay.

My last ever Sunday lunch was a dire affair. Had I known Eliza had invited the McKenzies, I would have cried off, but I had only seen her briefly when I had got back on Friday and collected Mildred. I didn't see her at all on Saturday. I really hated sharing a table with the man who I knew was likely to become my murderer. More so, I loathed sharing a table with the family I had to say goodbye to forever. In fact, I got so close to calling the whole plan off. I had known I would have terrible doubts, but once Bob had my letter, it had been too late. I had delivered it to the front door of the manor on Saturday afternoon. I knew the housekeeper acted like a butler as well as cook. She always answered the front door, which was seldom used except for formal occasions.

Once I had handed that letter over, for me there was no reprieve. When Bob had received it, he must have worked out that Jay was the best person to implicate. During lunch on Sunday, he deliberately turned the conversation to people's daily routines and Eliza mentioned that I was a creature of habit who walked Mildred on the same route every morning at about 9.30am.

Lingering over my grave at my funeral, my sorrow was overwhelming as I watched poor Eliza, Jay and the children sob their hearts out. I hurt so much for all of them. I had never even seen my first grandchild, Juliet, one last time before I left. I watched her blub and remembered her so well when she was little and how much I had cherished her arrival into the world.

I miss my family, my friends and I miss little Mildred. I want to cuddle and feed and walk and sleep with her. And poor Pam grieves over my death. I contemplated including her in my plan, but knew I could trust no-one to take on the huge responsibility of permitting my murder to go ahead. They could so easily have baulked at the last minute and ruined things. These questions bother me. They will not let me be. Should I have been braver and stayed alive as long as I could? Or did I do the right thing?

I watched the trial with fascination. McKenzie, of course, pleaded not guilty. Throughout the whole trial, his countenance showed not a hint of concern or remorse. In fact, he smiled a lot, as though he was amused by the wrongful absurdity of it all.

But a unanimous jury found him guilty. He has been put away where he belongs. I followed him to prison and have stayed to watch him adapt to the life there. As cunning and clever as they are, psychopaths cannot resist the fear and admiration of others. The need to be one up can be irresistible to them and so often proves their downfall.

I heard him brag to another prisoner how he detested and killed his wife's Chihuahua, and boast about how he dropped in on Francesca who, already drunk, was about to make a bacon sandwich. Too far gone to resist his kiss, he told her he had always wanted her, took her up to bed and had sex with her. Afterwards when she had passed out into a deep snoring sleep, he had slipped downstairs, turned on the gas flame under the pan with uncooked bacon in it. He had moved the J-cloths and kitchen roll close to the hob and slipped out quietly.

I was always in favour of the right to die by one's own choosing.

Regrets aside, I am lucky to have had the chance to be able to decide my own ending and to have accepted that fate before I left. Acceptance was what Bob craved, but altogether the wrong kind. I know that I am one of the lucky ones. Unlike too many hordes of babies, children, young adults born to live and die too fast, I was stopped late in the day after a good long game. But now it's enough. I need to cease remembering, loving and hating. I have come away from Bob. Eliza feels my love and is safe to leave, so with reluctance I have broken away from her too. My story is done. So now, the essence of my being can merge into the vast sea of vibrations that connects us all.